"The characters in these stories are the uprooted whose lives are defined by loss, betweenness, and unavoidable severance, and Mäkinen writes about their lives with tremendous care. These pages vibrate with deep resonance."

HA JIN
National Book Award-winning author of *A Song Everlasting* and *Waiting*

"*The Ghosts of Other Immigrants* is an exquisite collection that depicts the cosmic longing and disorientation of immigrants with stunning originality. History echoes in Maija Mäkinen's stories, singing of both beauty and wreckage. Both darkly funny and devastating, [these] stories reveal a fiercely insightful writer with a fully formed vision."

TSERING YANGZOM LAMA
Author of *We Measure the Earth with Our Bodies*

"*The Ghosts of Other Immigrants* describes the immigrant experience with humor, depth, and longing. Whether you're an immigrant from Finland or have never left your hometown, you will love and identify with the honest, complicated, and vulnerable women you will meet in this book."

MARIA KUZNETSOVA
Author of *Oksana, Behave!* and *Something Unbelievable*

THE GHOSTS OF OTHER IMMIGRANTS

THE GHOSTS OF OTHER IMMIGRANTS

STORIES

MAIJA MÄKINEN

newamericanpress

*

Milwaukee, Wisconsin

newamericanpress

Printed in the United States of America
ISBN 978-1-941561-29-4

Cover + Book Design by Angelo Maneage

For ordering information, please contact:
Ingram Book Group
One Ingram Blvd.
La Vergne, TN 37086
(800) 937-8000
orders@ingrambook.com

For media and event inquiries, please visit:
www.newamericanpress.com

CONTENTS

MONKEY BARS   9

1993   31

VIRGINIA BEACH   51

STETSON GIRL   55

BALLERINA DREAMS   81

COUNTRY FICTION   85

P.S. KATE   107

THE GHOSTS OF
OTHER IMMIGRANTS   129

CALDERAS   133

YELLOWSTONE   151

SHE AND SIBELIUS   159

MONKEY BARS

THE WASHINGTON AIR BRIMMED OVER, frothed almost. It filled our mouths and stomachs and tickled our skin to soft submission as soon as we stepped off the plane. We took a deep breath and gave in.

It was August. The four of us—me, my brother and our parents—stood in the short-term parking lot at Dulles Airport. A yolk-colored sun simmered in the dirty horizon, slender stretches of cloud, like liquefying pewter, stretched across it. The sky was the sheen of Teflon and the air so hot it quivered, making the planes taking off and landing look like they were melting.

We watched the sooty back end of the airport bus that had just dropped us off disappearing into the distance. The airport was bigger than anything I had ever seen and filled with cars, hundreds, thousands of them.

"What's this smell, daddy," I asked.

He sniffed. "It's relative humidity. It's the smell of America."

The air did smell of America: of cars, metal, rubber, gasoline. We followed my father who strode ahead with the two biggest suitcases. He flung his head from side to side, pointing out different makes of cars: Buick, Chevrolet, Ford… "And that—that is a Cadillac."

He pronounced it *cad-el-laakh*, twanging it like an American. The rest of us smiled in wonder. *Cad*-el-laahhkhh. Then he stopped and sat down on the low hood of a huge white car. Our car. It had been discussed at length during expensive trans-Atlantic phone calls, my mother poring over brochures while my father visited D.C. dealerships. He spread out his arms. "Ta-da!"

The silence that followed was full of the thunder and boom of the airport. I wondered what 'ta-da' meant. My mother said the car was too big and I saw my father's shoulders slouch.

The drive to our new house in the new car was long. Darkness had fallen and I watched the whites of my father's eyes dart between the highway, the rearview mirror and my mother. My brother Risto had fallen asleep with his thumb in his mouth, but I was glued to the flood-lit four-lane highway, and the cement barrier separating us from another four lanes going in the opposite direction. In Finland we only had two-lane highways. Eight seemed dangerous.

After the exit everything turned quiet. We drove through leafy, suburban streets lined with houses whose windows were lit yellow and came to a stop in the corner of two streets. My father turned off the engine and indicated the house on top of the little hill next to where we had parked. A single window was illuminated. Across the street, there was only darkness and tall trees.

We were all silent: this was the moment of truth. When we opened the doors now, the big change would be a reality.

"Your school is back there, behind those trees," said my father who had noticed the direction of my gaze. He opened the door and we heard the crickets and cicadas for the first time, but I was fixated on the school, invisible behind the black tree trunks. School would start in a week. My stomach cramped in a hot twist. In Finland, school was a ten-minute walk from our house. This was much too close.

My father hauled suitcases up the steps to the house while Risto and I stood uncertainly on the edge of the sidewalk, gazing at a long gap that gaped open in the curb. It was at least one meter wide. I crouched down to look inside. A sewer maybe? I stuck in my hand, and the air inside the concrete hole felt different than the outside air, cold and threatening.

"Careful! American sewers are big, they can swallow little children."

We retreated to the grassy hill, where sparks lit up the air. "Daddy, daddy, sparks! There's a fire!" I had once seen with my grandmother an old factory burn down in the center of our hometown.

My father smiled. "Those aren't sparks. They're fireflies."

We stood in silence looking for the yellow specks of lights to appear and listening to the crickets up in the trees. I had never heard anything like it—like the aural equivalent of a sky thick with stars.

For a long time, the four of us stood in the velvety dark, sinking into America.

—

In the morning my brother and I explored the house. My bedroom and the bathroom were facing the school, which I now saw had a red-brick façade.

Behind the house was a backyard with patchy lawn and a single shrubby tree near the chain-link fence between us and the neighbor. We crept under the low-hanging branches where the air smelled of shadow and soil. The ground was brown, almost orange, not black like at home, and dry. When I stomped my feet, I heard a thump instead of the familiar soft thud. We poked at the dirt with a stick. How could anything grow in this?

The neighbors had an elaborate swing set, with a regular swing, a baby swing and a swing that was a horse, like something on a carousel. On one end of the structure was a trellis for climbing and on the other a plastic playhouse. We were agog—we hadn't even known it was possible to have your *own*, personal swing set.

A door opened and a boy shouted: "Nadya!"

A fluffy white dog came careening across the yard, and at its heels a small boy with straight, dark hair. A moment later, a slightly older girl with a long, golden ponytail and pink bow strolled into the yard. The dog squatted in a far corner of the yard, shitting. Risto and I were frozen in position under the tree, watching the dog finish and start raking the dirt with its white paws. Then it ambled across the yard, wagging its tail, and sat down in front of us on the other side of the chain link fence. A woman came out, carrying both a baby and a tray with tall glasses of red juice. We could hear the ice cubes clinking in the glasses. As the boy and girl ran up to take a glass, the woman looked around for the dog and saw us under the tree. She smiled and waved the empty tray in the air.

She was straight out of a comic, like Super-Woman: scalloped waist, wide hips, pointy breasts. Her white angora wool sweater was pure dream. And her hair. It was fabulous. She had incised a sharp dividing line precisely in the middle of her head, and on either side of it a swell of bleached hair gleamed frozen in hairspray. I lifted my hand in greeting and followed Risto, already retreating to the safety of the kitchen.

—

On the first day of fourth grade at Kensington Elementary School it immediately became apparent that it was a mistake to have the last name Horsma.

Ms. Melligan ("Mzzz," she had said to me when introducing herself, "not *miss*!"), our fresh-faced twenty-two-year-old teacher, stood in front of the class. She had long, dark-brown hair and a heart-shaped face and wore a short dress that left most of her bare legs visible.

"Girls and boys, I want us to say hello to Saila Horsma, she is going to be in our class this year. She comes all the way from Finland! Say hello to Saila!"

She pronounced my name 'sailuh,' the way a New Jerseyan would say 'sailor.'

The class yelled in unison, but I heard snickering from amongst the boys, and a skinny girl in the front row turned around and made a face at me. There were whispers.

"Whore-sma!"

"Sailah Whore-sma."

"Sailah whore's ma favorite whore!"

It made no difference that I didn't properly understand the meaning of the words; the tone of the messages was familiar and clear from my school in Finland: *you* are pathetic, fat and a crybaby. *Loser*.

I cried over my desk all day long in the first weeks, a sea of tears on the icy-grey Formica. I wept uncontrollably, inconsolably, pathologically, with such force that at times my crying muscles would contract and seize so that I couldn't stop even when I tried. I watched the rest of the class from behind my long hair, hidden and imprisoned all at once, a strange satellite of despair in the midst of the normalcy of daily life—other people's normalcy—and refused to put pen to paper. And with the desk welling with salt water, I couldn't lift my head when the crying did cease, and I cowered wetly behind my hair, waiting for the next break or lunch, when everyone left the classroom except for Ms. Melligan, who would come over and set a stack of yellow hand towels on the edge of my desk so that I could clean up the mess.

During the lunch break I sat in the library reading along with several other solitary children, while the rest ran around in the school yard, dangled off the monkey bars or played tetherball.

—

That year, it was a fashion among the girls to buy "Scratch 'n Sniff" notebooks with scented pictures on the cover. The strawberry smelled of strawberry, the fruit candy of candy, but the most popular scent was Strawberries and Cream. But the only Scratch 'n Sniff notebook remaining in the store when we went had a slice of pizza, smelling of pepperoni and chemical oregano.

"Eww, you have pizza on your notebook," taunted the skinny girl whose name was Daniela.

"Daniela," Ms. Melligan warned.

"Don't mind her, she's stupid," Dorrie said. She had an unscented picture of a race car on her notebook. She glared at Daniela, who sashayed back to her own desk, swinging her straight brown hair from side to side.

I had the typical seventies Finnish Cold War girl hair, cut straight across the forehead a hairsbreadth above the eyebrows and equally unswervingly across the upper back, washed a couple of times a week. But in America children were bathed every night before bed. Daniela told me so and shrieked in disgusted delight when she discovered that I wasn't. "*My* mommy gives me a bath every night. Yours doesn't? Gross!"

"Daniela." Ms. Melligan kept an eye but also her distance. She had stopped bringing over the hand towels so that I had to get up and go get them myself from above the sink at the front of the class. She no longer knelt by my desk to talk to me, had stopped consoling me, and sensing that I had gone too far, cried too much, the tears dried up.

—

"Dad, it's my turn tomorrow to bring in the khurnevens."

"Khurne-what?"

"Khurnevens, khurnevens!"

In the morning he walked me to class to consult Ms. Melligan. "Saila tells me that she must bring to school something like khurnevens?"

"Current events?"

'Current events' was part of the syllabus and required everyone to bring in a newspaper clipping on a topical issue and present the news item in front of the class.

Prisoners and immigrants learn quickly to survive by seeking the protection of the strongest and most dangerous member of a group, and cunningly I brought a story about Daniela's idol, the figure skater Dorothy Hamill. Daniela sat silent as I stumbled through the few sentences I had prepared, and at lunch she sat down next to me. She had been warming up to me, against her will it seemed, and all of a sudden we became "best friends."

We now exchanged notes in the pizza notebook about brown-eyed Bates and jerk-off Jeff.

Me: *Do you wish to kiss Bates?*

Daniela: *Of course.*

Me: *So do I! I love him*

Daniela: *Me too.*

In a matter of months, I was transformed from an unfashionable, non-English-speaking foreign crybaby "whoresma" with a pepperoni notebook, to an exotic *somebody* who spoke weird English, knew previously unknown things, and whose wardrobe slowly grew to acceptable bounds and whose hair now received the required daily washing.

—

There had been kidnappings of children in the D.C. area, and my parents and the neighbors had agreed that all four children should play together despite our age differences, to make it easier to keep track of us. We were supposed to stay in the backyard and keep the gate latched and never go out into the street.

Unbeknownst to them, we often played on the wrong side of the fence, in the shaded corridor between the chain link fence and the cedar bushes growing behind it, on the street side. We were out of sight of the kitchen windows of both houses as well as from the street and could easily get there through a gate in the fence.

"Shazam!" I got into a fighting stance under the cedars.

As the oldest, Amanda the neighbor girl and I had hijacked both of the leading roles from the boys.

Amanda leapt from under a cedar bush. "He strikes down the bad guy!"

"Heeelp," Ryan screamed.

"Shhh! Not so loud, Mommy will hear," she warned her brother. We listened.

"Ryan? Amanda?"

The bell on Nadya's collar tinkled nearby. Her speckled-caramel snout appeared in the bushes on the neighbor's side and she wagged her tail happily at us.

Belinda's blonde head appeared among the branches. She pinched her pink lips together and vanished. Moments later her front door closed with a bang and we saw her scaling the small hill between the sidewalk and the hedge, the baby under her arm. Ryan and Amanda crawled out of the bushes and followed her as she rounded the corner to our front door. Risto and I meandered back to our yard through the gate and waited until we saw my mother's face in the plastic window of the screen door. She jabbed it open with an angry finger, then crooked it to indicate *get in*.

We were not allowed to play with Amanda and Ryan for a month.

—

"So what, they're too young anyway," I said to Risto.

He was five and didn't see my point, but at ten, I felt the seven-year-old Amanda was too young for me.

"Let's play barbies."

Sitting on the floor in front of his bed, Risto gripped the cinnamon-colored GI Joe, naked apart from molded-on plastic shorts. I held a naked Domino and Daisy doll.

"GI Joe is coming over!"

"Hey Joe… let's go to the sauna, it's sauna night."

Risto and I often played with my barbies. Sometimes Amanda and I had played with them, but although she appreciated my European dolls, with their smaller breasts, narrow hips and bendable arms and legs—hers all looked like Belinda—I had shocked her by insisting that they all go into the sauna, together with G.I. Joe, with no clothes on.

She objected to his presence.

"But it is sauna—all go, women and men," I said.

"What's a sauna?"

"Hot room."

"Why is she on top of him?"

I remembered the day Ryan had burst out of their backdoor, screaming: *I saw my sister naked! I saw my sister naked!* Risto and I had looked at each other and agreed wordlessly that we would never tell our American friends that we had seen everybody naked—family, relatives, friends—before or after the sauna. I thought Amanda was hopelessly innocent. I had *always* known that men and women went to a sauna together and sometimes had sex.

Risto dumped his toys out of the red plastic laundry hamper that served as the sauna and set it on its side. We sat the dolls down inside the basket.

"Let's put them on top of each other."

I took the GI Joe from Risto and ground the girl dolls against him one at a time. Their plastic limbs made clicking, knocking sounds. "Ok. Now they're going to a party. They're gonna wear ball gowns. You can take Daisy." We chose dresses from a pile of handmade barbie clothes that my mother had sewed out of leftover fabric.

"She's not wearing that," I remarked as Risto struggled to pull a brown dress over Daisy. "She's wearing that one." I pointed to a pale-blue evening gown. On Domino I put a red sequin dress, factory made and therefore superior.

"They're going to a party," Risto repeated. He was threading Daisy's clubfoot, molded in the shape of a high-heeled shoe, into a tiny pink plastic pump.

"Daisy doesn't have shoes, Domino does." I took the shoes from him. I tore off Domino's ball gown. "It's the next day. We're having a big party." I wiggled Domino's hips the same way I sometimes practiced myself. I was Domino, on my way to meet Bates. I found a striped shirt for GI Joe, similar to the ones Bates wore, and took him from Risto.

—

There were frozen vegetables floating in the toilet water. I had excused myself from the dinner table and had just spat them out of my cheek, where I had slowly stored them all through eating. I couldn't stand American frozen vegetables, the freeze-dried carrot chips and the horrid, pale floury lima beans, drifting intact among the disintegrating mush in the toilet.

The foam filling inside the toilet-seat cushion sighed softly when I leaned against it with my elbows. The familiar Washington smell of rain falling on warm grass wafted in through the open window. I liked spending time in the bathroom, a spacious room with a picture window facing the street. I could hardly remember the narrow water closet back home, built in the 1950s, windowless, utilitarian, dreary. In this bathroom the window let in western light and the bottom half showed the top of a rose bush. The thorny branches were scratching the window. A storm was rising, and fat drops began to hit the glass.

I flushed and climbed up on the fur-covered toilet seat to see myself in the mirror. I thought I was fairly womanly already, fairly mature. I flung my hair over my shoulder and smiled seductively, like women on television. My hair shone with the daily washing with Head 'n Shoulders and from brushing it afterwards, to match the shampoo ad on television. I had no idea it was a dandruff shampoo.

But no matter how I brushed, I couldn't get my hair to gleam in the way that Daniela, for example, managed with her long straight hair, shiny like polyester and cut in the style of Dorothy Hamill. In America, a girl's hair had to shine like a doll's. They even sold a doll without a body—the torso-less Crissy doll was only a head with long, russet hair that you could brush and curl. *Beautiful hair makes a girl look beautiful*, a soft woman's voice said in the television ad.

Under my shirt I felt the downy cotton of my training bra. I had convinced my parents to get one after seeing them in a Sears catalog on girls even younger than myself. It made me feel secret and strong, even though some of the girls at school had made fun of me for it. I had been walking back to class after lunch when a fifth-grade girl stopped me in the hallway. I didn't know her, but knew of her, because little girls always know who the older girls are. I was alone, maybe Daniela and Dorrie were both absent on the same day, but I was more confident by now and wasn't intimidated by walking alone. Perhaps my assurance had brimmed over and I was actually swinging my hips a little as I walked, maybe I had thrust out my chest a little, the little nubs, light as feathers, encased in the new trainer bra.

The fifth-grader asked if I was really wearing a bra and I said yes, I was. She seemed delighted and hurried off down the hall.

The next day at morning assembly everyone seemed to know that "that foreign girl" wore a bra. A group of girls approached me and one of them asked why I wore one when I had nothing to show. Others whispered and giggled, shooting glances at my chest. The boys were kinder. They seemed respectful, even a little frightened, and excited. Many said hello to me as we all walked back to our classrooms.

What kept me going and convinced me not to abandon the bra was this: that morning, walking to class, Bates smiled at me for the first time.

To seal our friendship, Daniela and I had decided we both had a crush on him, even though it was me who'd had an eye on him since the beginning of the school year.

Bates was clean, well-behaved and brown-eyed and usually paid no attention to me, only joked around with Daniela. But Daniela was flat as a board and though I didn't have much, I had *something*.

I imagined Bates taking my hand—and then… I wasn't sure.

I looked out the bathroom window. The rain was pouring down by now.

My parents and Risto were in the living room eating chocolate Jell-o and watching Sonny and Cher. "I got you, babe," she sang, and I imagined her extending her long arms above her head. "I got you, babe," I whispered in between spoonfuls of Jell-o.

—

It was spring now, but the shadows reaching across the schoolyard were still cold once the sun had disappeared behind the woods.

The wind was rising. I stood by myself next to the monkey bars in the school playground. With one hand I held onto the iron bar, up to my hips. I got up on my toes so that the bar touched my pelvis and, head down, folded my body over, too slowly this time, and collapsed on my back onto the hard ground, chewed up and bald after years of children kicking off from the monkey bars.

My father should have come for me already. The tree shadows were getting longer and longer, they had long since swallowed the monkey bars and already covered most of the rest of the schoolyard. Crickets and cicadas had started chirping and the cedar fence that circled the schoolgrounds looked like a black, impenetrable ring.

Lying on the hard-packed earth I heard the burble of the nearby creek, leading to Rock Creek Park. The creek wound through the woods, lapping its silty tongue against the pale roots of smooth tree trunks, their roots like knobby witch's claws pinching the earth. The creek ended in a park where my family often went on Sunday picnics, along the pantyhose-brown shores of the Potomac. I thought of the sandwiches with sliced turkey, American cheese, iceberg lettuce and Thousand Island dressing and felt hungry.

I could see the treetops curling above the cedar fence in the direction of the creek. In daylight they were just trees, but with shadows attached to their trunks and hollows, and the darkness blowing in, they looked forbidding. I didn't have the courage to dive through the cedars alone, so I got back onto the monkey bars, to separate myself from the cooling ground.

I gripped the bar and flung one leg over it and held onto the bar with one hand, sniffing the other: the familiar smell of sharp metal. The skin on my palms had turned red, hot and tender from the friction, blisters were beginning to form. I threw my throbbing hand in the air, like a rodeo star, and straightened my legs, straight as scissors, and pitched forward so that the force of my weight and the velocity pivoted me back into an upright position. Over and over again, pitch forward, swing back, pause; earth, grass, woods' edge, black sky, earth. I closed my eyes and let go, let the motion take care of itself, spinning blindly again and again.

"Saila!"

Woods' edge, cedar and sky melded into one another as I was flung onto the hard earth. I saw my father running across the grass. He reached me and pulled me up and held my shoulders until my eyes had stopped rolling and everything was steady again.

We listened to the crickets. The air smelled of America.

—

Before spring break Bates casually walked over to my desk one morning, before Ms. Melligan was in the classroom.

My heart pounded. Bates didn't usually approach me voluntarily. It was happening, at last. He was interested in me!

"Hey Saila, I wanted to ask you something."

"Ok."

Kids were still filing in noisily, the well-behaved ones already pulling out their copies of *My Favorite Reading Comprehension*. Ms. Melligan appeared at the door to hurry the stragglers along. Bates glanced behind him, at his friends Jason and Holland, who were grinning.

"I was just wondering—would you want to strip for me today after school?"

What was 'strip' again? Or had I ever even heard of it? I was doing all right in class by now, and more importantly, during recess, but I still ran into situations like this every day. 'Strip' must have been a game we had played in school, I decided; I must have just forgotten its name. Whatever, I thought, I didn't care what we played. But I played it safe. "I don't know."

"You don't know?"

"Uhm, ok."

"Really? You're gonna strip for me?"

"Yeah, ok."

"Ok. I'll come to your house after school."

"Ok."

At home I immediately began to doubt whether Bates would show up, but I told my mother that someone from school might come by to play. At the same time I hoped that he wouldn't come, after all.

From the bathroom window I watched the crossing guards leave their posts at the street corner at three-thirty. Moments later I saw Bates at the street corner one block away, with two other boys. I got a sick feeling of disappointment.

Still, when the doorbell rang, I was trembling with excitement. What could we do?

My mother opened the door. The two boys with Bates turned out to be Jason and Holland, even though I had never even talked to them. Bates looked wound up, but he maintained his manners. "Hello Mrs. Horsma, it's nice to meet you. My name is Bates."

Jason and Holland seemed awkward as my mother greeted them and I stood in the middle of the living room, red-faced. Did we want some juice, my mother wanted to know. The boys said no, and she herded us off into the kitchen, toward the backyard.

I led the three of them out through the screen door and racked my brain for something we could do. There were Risto's toys in the sandbox, but we were a bit old for them. Or I could get the badminton rackets from inside. Or something. Bates smiled. "So. You want to do it?"

"What?"

"You're gonna strip?"

"Ok."

"Ok."

"Ok."

I ran back inside. "Mom, what does 'strip' mean?"

She looked at me thoughtfully. Right then my father came in

through the front door, briefcase in hand. "Hey, what does 'strip' mean again?"

"It's to remove something, like paint. Or to undress."

"Like take off your clothes?"

A ballast of lead fell and burned the bottom of my stomach.

My parents wrested the story out of me, and before I could stop him, my father was striding through the kitchen and into the backyard. The aluminum screen door shrieked and slammed against the frame and I could hear the bass highlights of his voice for a long time, followed by a heavy silence. Then, they all filed into the living room, my father shooing Bates and his mute companions ahead of him.

He forced each one of the boys to give up their home phone number, underlined the severity of the issue once more, and sent them home. Bates wouldn't even look at me.

I was mortified. I wanted to die and stop going to school and move back to Finland. Number one: I hadn't understood what Bates had said to me. Number two: I had agreed to "it." Three: Bates had brought two other boys with him! Four: I had gone back on my promise to him. Five: my parents now knew the whole story. Six: my father had yelled at the boy I was in love with. Seven: after spring break, I would have to go back to school, where my big love and his minions would be in the same classroom with me all day and every day for the rest of the interminable school year.

—

After spring break, Bates said nothing about the incident, but treated me coolly, from a distance. One day after school, walking home toward the intersection where we parted ways, I was slightly up ahead of him, but I knew that he was right behind me. I dawdled on purpose so that he would have to pass me and we could say hello. I smiled shyly when he passed.

"Why are you always smiling," he snapped and barged past me.

—

By the end of the school year, in June, Bates had softened towards me again, and one Friday he asked if I would perhaps like to kiss him after school. We could meet in the playground, he said, and I made a vague promise.

In my room at home after school I weighed the matter and, at the appointed time, scanned from the bathroom window the stretch of parkland along the street in front of the schoolyard. Somewhere behind those trees he might be waiting already. Would I go? All year I had dreamed about this. I had never kissed anyone.

A little before four, while my mother and Risto were in the backyard, I opened the front door and crossed the street to the park. Immediately I could see Bates through the trees, meandering near the monkey bars. I turned around.

I berated myself. At last he had come around, at last he liked me, wanted a kiss. I didn't give him one. Why not? I didn't trust that it was all right, and besides, we were leaving anyway. Plus after the stripping episode I didn't have the courage. What if it was just a joke? What if Bates laughed when I showed up? Maybe Jason and Holland would jump out of the bushes and fall all over themselves laughing, or maybe it would be a group of older girls, fifth- or sixth-graders, who would hold me down and take off my bra?

I crept up to the cedar fence where we had played Shazam and Isis, and waited until my mother and Risto went inside. I snuck in after them, listening in the kitchen as she talked to him in the bathroom, where he liked to accompany her. I slipped in behind the basement door and waited on the topmost step until I heard her calling me, and opened the door, pretending I had been in the basement the whole time.

I went into the bathroom and locked the door and climbed back on the edge of the tub, waiting for Bates to appear between the trees. He would have to cross the street on his way home.

He hadn't appeared yet when my mother knocked on the door and told me to come help her with the dinner. Maybe he had left while I was lying in wait under the cedars, waiting for my mother and Risto to go inside.

—

Bates wasn't in school on Monday. It's because of me, I thought, he must be really mad. I was worried too; there was only a week of school left and I had to see him again.

He didn't come the next day either.

On the third day Ms. Melligan called us to order in the morning. She looked serious. Bates' desk was empty again. Daniela looked at me and raised her eyebrows.

"Class. I have something very sad to tell all of you this morning. I have spoken with some of your parents and together we have decided that it would be best to tell you some bad news before you hear it from somewhere else. Today, when you go home, your parents will talk to you about it more. For now, I will say only that one of your classmates..." Ms. Melligan's voice broke and she looked down. "... is not coming back."

Dusty silence. A cold sweat appeared on my skin, and I felt sick.

"The most important thing is to remember that we have all been very lucky that we have known Bates. And what's even more important is that you NEVER EVER leave your house alone, unattended, under any circumstances, no matter what. Is that clear?"

"Yes Ms. Melligan!"

"What do we say? 'Never...'"

"Never go alone!"

I was frozen with terror and confusion. It had to be my fault, I had done it, done something terrible. I should have known that something was wrong when I didn't see Bates come out of the trees that night. I should have kissed him. I was furious with myself. Now I would probably go to jail, an American jail.

But the policeman who came to our classroom during lunch that day asked me nothing and spent most of his time talking to Jason and Holland and a few other boys. Bates must not have told anyone that he was going to meet me. It was our secret. It hadn't been a joke.

—

A week later, before July 4th, America's Bicentennial, which we had talked about at school all year long, we stood in a passenger terminal at the port of Montreal in front of a wall of windows and watched an enormous pair of pliers clamp around the big white car, lifting it up from the loading area over a length of roiling sea, and through a dark opening on the deck of the ship.

"Saila won't be here then," Ms. Melligan had said many times over the spring, whenever we had discussed the Bicentennial. She would always smile sadly, and my classmates would turn in their seats and regard me with pity and wonder.

I longed to be back in Washington, to feel under my hand the red dirt, where I imagined Bates buried. Traces of that soil were still visible in the engravings of my sneakers.

Before our departure, as we had cleaned the house, I had snatched the broom from my mother, who was sweeping the hardened patch of ground in front of the kitchen door so briskly that I felt offended. Gently, I stroked the dirt with the tips of the bristles. There you are, I thought, there you are.

Daniela and I said goodbye on the last day of class. We

were supposed to have a going-away party for me, but Bates' disappearance made it seem improper, and Ms. Melligan just gave a short speech at the end of the day and wished me well. Daniela said she would visit me in Finland as soon as we were teenagers. Amanda and Ryan and Nadya came out to wave goodbye, with Belinda watching from the doorway.

From Montreal, the ship, one of the last passenger ships to cross the Atlantic between the old and new continents, headed to the Atlantic and then eastward to Rotterdam. Risto and I got seasick in the first meters as the ship began to shudder and heave in the ocean. We had to forgo the elaborate dinners and never saw the sumptuous ice sculptures decking the dining room tables, hearing about them only from my parents who returned each night with saltines and orange soda obtained from the waiter.

On the top bunk of the cabin I dreamed of the edge of a woods. I walked into the trees, went in deeper and deeper and felt desire rise within me, for the first time. Despite my age I recognized it immediately. It began somewhere behind my hips and abdomen, in a dark place. I walked and walked, and the deeper into the woods I went, the greater the desire I felt. Too late. Looking out over the grey waters of the Atlantic through the porthole, I held in my hand a heart-shaped Valentine, which read: "To Seighla from Bates S". The surface of the ocean was so close to the window of our lower-tier cabin that sometimes all I could see was water, as if looking beneath the surface of the earth.

When my father took me up to the foredeck at night to get some fresh air, I held onto the railing white-knuckled, my ankles pressed into the metal of the bottom rung, knees scraping the thick rope suspended between the top and bottom. Sickeningly, the rope gave way a little. There was no deck below to break a fall, only a dead drop down the ship's steely side. Falling would mean plunging into the resounding, black depths of the Atlantic.

The motion of the ship from the bottom of a wave was slow

and ponderous. It creaked in its joints as it climbed, grumbling and rising, cresting, and for a terrible moment the ocean vanished from view altogether and all my father and I saw was the shuddering bow etched against a sky of oxidized silver, until the vessel seesawed, plunging, the bow slicing into the trough of waves, and it felt as if nothing could prevent the ship from charging all the way down, into the depths of the ocean, and never coming back up again.

TAIMI WAS EIGHTY-TWO, but on her way home from the village grocery, as she looked upon the fat border of lupine along the dirt lane, she was reminded of being ten years old and seeing the painting of the Queen of Sweden for the first time at the Viipuri art museum.

The museum was now on the other side, in Russia, and her hometown no longer part of Finland. She felt the old paralyzing grief despite the five decades that had passed since her evacuation from the darkened city. Five decades, yet she had never stopped seeing signs of Viipuri in her day-to-day life. It was as if everything that was to happen to her over the ensuing years had been set forth in that microcosm of youth in Viipuri—as if a crystal spinning in the July breeze had caught the pink, purple and blue of the lupines frothing atop one another on this Southern Finland roadside, that vision containing behind it the other one, of the thick flounces at the Queen's throat in the Viipuri museum.

It was the same Queen whose visit to Viipuri in the 1600s had left in its wake the rumor that the royal had been found in the Round Tower in a compromising situation with another woman. Taimi had been in her middle years and the town had already been lost when the significance of those words had finally surfaced.

She glanced down at her own flounceless dress, chosen for the task of walking the bicycle to the store and back: a utilitarian beige polyamide with a brown jute-weave pattern down the front. Over her shoulders she had the blue sleeveless cardigan she'd crocheted herself, and on her feet the lumpy tan shoes that appeared and disappeared in her line of vision as she looked down past her breasts. *Those.* Her eye skated around the left one, the one with the problem inside that was now visible even on the outside.

She stopped at the mailboxes, and her heart fluttered as she thought of the letter from a week earlier. The American-flag stamps had made her think it was one of her youngest grandchild's quirky missives from Texas, but instead of Silja's glitter-dusted rainbow stationery and girlish cursive, the envelope had been a ladylike lavender with a typed address. Also, Silja was in Finland, staying with her, not in Texas.

No, it was only the newspaper this early in the day, carrying jubilant updates of Russian *glasnost* and *perestroika*. The fresh ink was oily on her fingers as she slipped the newspaper into the basket alongside the box with the chocolate pinecone cake, Silja's favorite. The teenager was probably still asleep in the parlor, dreaming of her American boyfriend. She had arrived looking like a Charlie's Angel, hair feathered, eyes rimmed with makeup, writing love letters "back home" and throwing herself into secret, gyrating dances in the garden when she thought no one was looking.

From the hilltop, Taimi looked down into the valley, at her own cottage and the half dozen others on her side of the sound. The sun flickering through the birches, the brief summer paradise of apple trees and kitchen gardens, and the fir trees quavering with thrush—someday soon Silja would return to this same view on another visit from America, and she, Taimi, would no longer be here.

The pain of her granddaughter's future sadness pierced her, but Silja couldn't be spared. No one could. At least she would never endure what Taimi's generation had endured—war, refugee lines, always living within earshot of the Soviet propaganda machine that, even after the war, had remained a palpable presence in Cold War Finland. Even in 1993, Taimi had no faith in the new "free" Russia that was supposed to be emerging. She was no fan of America, but maybe Silja was better off there, far from the enemy and safe from the interference of Russia in her destiny.

She had only a few more days left with her granddaughter. To make the most of it, she had bought an extra box of butter cookies, for the special vigil she had planned for tonight—a vigil to witness the blossoming of the night-blooming cereus. *Queen of the night*, her friend Ester had called it. Ester had transported the plant on the bus in her overnight knapsack, the leaf stem soaking in a clump of wet sand in a zip lock bag. It only opened its petals in the dark, Ester said, suggestively, and they had laughed long and deliciously, the way they did, acknowledging things that didn't need saying.

Now Ester, like Viktor, was gone. Taimi was the only one left of their war-ravaged generation. The old grocer had died the year before—she looked at the nice bone for marrow soup that his son had given her for nothing. *Old bones taste better*, he had said, winking one of his blue eyes. The original grocer used to look down on her and Viktor and the other Karelian refugees who had bought plots around the sound, after Viipuri was annexed to Russia. Government coercion, the grocer said about the land purchases; war veteran subsidy, she and Viktor said.

She had been in her twenties when she was evacuated west with everyone else, in the odd year of 1939, dragging two toddlers and a bundle of china and family photographs. Over the decades, she had learned to love this place that she at first couldn't fathom belonging to, nor it to her. Now it was all she had.

She patted the parcel of butcher paper with the bone. If she and this place didn't belong together by now, what did?

The pale band on her left ring finger, where her wedding and engagement rings had been, glowed a sickly white. She had taken the rings off for housework that morning, and removing them today, on the even-numbered 60th anniversary of her engagement to Viktor, seemed like an affront to him. But no one else would remember the anniversary—only Ester would have.

That the cereus was set to blossom on the anniversary of her engagement to Viktor did not surprise her. Ester, unmarried, had always had a presence in their marriage, and she would be pleased to be making an appearance on this night.

—

In the parlor, the pale green tapestry was aglow in the morning light sifting through the bay windows. In front of the center pane, in a place of honor on the bureau, was the cereus, its long, waxy leaves shaped like oars, the older ones dark green and limp on the lace doily, the newer ones almost incandescent and arching sinuously in all directions.

Right away she saw that the plant had changed overnight. The faintly penile sheaths that would become the flowers had grown longer and formed blooms resembling stringy little mops. She wanted to touch one but restrained herself lest she interrupt some sensitive pre-blossoming process. She turned to the spectacle of her granddaughter.

The half-naked Silja, shifting her hips in Taimi's dowry linens and drawing long, heavy breaths, was infusing the room with the fumes of her teenage fertility. She was dressed in a scant outfit with shorts and no sleeves, like a baby's onesie. The day before, when Taimi came in to check whether the cereus was making the little snapping sounds Ester had said signaled the plant was ready to bloom, she had found Silja lying in a position she wished it were possible to forget: half under the red satin quilt and splayed diagonally across a tangle of embroidered sheets, one hand cradling her pubic bone inside her underwear. Taimi hadn't known what to do—whenever Silja had touched herself as a little girl, she had swatted her hand away, the same as with her own children.

She averted her eyes from her granddaughter's bare thighs; thighs she had seen hundreds of times. "Wake up," she said and turned back to the plant.

Silja began her long, slow process of yawning and moaning, and came to stand next to her, stretching her downy limbs. "It doesn't look very exotic."

"Don't judge a book by its cover." Silja, half a head taller than her now, had brought down her arms so that the fading red mark on her neck was right in front of Taimi's eyes. She smacked her lips in distaste and swatted her granddaughter on the shoulder, not hard, but with purpose. Silja's eyes widened, but she knew what the swat was about. This girl, who'd spent every summer here since she was born, was no longer the child to whom she had read stories about witches and wizards and princesses who gazed into ponds, and to whom she had recited the proverbs and life lessons she had learned in Karelia. *If you fall, you'll break your bones. People don't fly, birds do.* Silja had especially loved the song about Tirlittan, the girl who climbed into a tree, fell, died, was buried, and rotted away. "*Tirlittan kiipes puuhun, Tirlittan putosi...*" Taimi hummed.

"*Tirlittan kuoli ja kuopattiin, Tirlittan mätäni!*" Silja put her usual relish on the last word, "rotted." Seconds later she was in the yard, skipping along the dirt path to the outhouse. Not skipping—twisting her body this way and that, dancing as she went. After she disappeared from view behind the black currant bushes, the gap at the top of the outhouse doorway showed that she had left the door open. Viktor had set the privy in the farthest corner of the garden to conceal both the odor and the user from the house, making it possible to leave the door ajar. "There will be no shitting in the dark in this house," he used to say to make the girls laugh. His other oft-repeated joke—"I made everything in this house myself—except the old lady"—had annoyed her. She had worked alongside him to construct the cottage, and it was she who had commissioned most of the items he had made, she who had carried the girls to term. She was the one who "made" them.

The telephone rang in the kitchen. She ran, gripped by the anxiety she felt whenever the apparatus came alive. She hated telephones, there had been none in her youth; only wealthy people and businessmen made telephone calls. She grasped the green receiver and waited for the person on the other end to speak.

"Mother?"

It was her youngest, Anneli, sounding different now that she wasn't calling from Texas. *How can you leave your homeland, the land your father almost died for!* she had cried when Anneli announced she and Heino were moving to America to teach at a university. Taimi had never liked the husband, who spoke to her as though she were a nice dog and who was always flicking back his blond, movie-star hair. He was a geneticist, like Anneli—both of her daughters were experts in things whose names she barely understood. "What time are you coming," she asked Anneli for the sake of saying something; she had never mastered the art of telephone conversation.

"I thought we were supposed to be there at two."

We meant Heino was coming too. The two of them sitting next to each other, skinny as reeds, drinking their coffee black and surgically removing the fat from the cured ham on her buttered slices of bread. She had even caught Anneli scraping the butter off the bread and folding it into her napkin. How quickly they had forgotten the years of malnourishment and food rations.

"How is it going with Silja?" Anneli was asking.

"You better keep a close watch on that girl." She debated whether to bring up the too-revealing clothing.

"Why? What did she do?"

The front step creaked; Silja had gone back to the parlor. Taimi watched as a magpie shot through the cherry trees and into the lilac orchard, scattering a family of starlings. The starlings chattered, darting from tree to tree. A few settled on the lower limbs of the old maple she and Viktor had planted. She unlatched the window and stuck her head out. Insects buzzed. The magpie was now in the red elderberry, the "shit tree," they called it in Karelia, it made you sick to your stomach but you could cure rickets with it. During the war, she had wrapped its leaves around the malnourished Anneli's bent little legs, to straighten them.

"Mother? Are you there?"

Anneli's tinny voice crackled in the receiver. These moments were happening more and more—it was like a sudden loss of frequency. How long had it been? Just the thought about the elderberry, or more than that? Impossible to trace after the fact. "Till two o'clock, then. Goodbye," she said cordially and replaced the receiver in its cradle.

She had her ear to the ring dial, to make sure the apparatus had gone silent, when Silja came in. "Did you latch the outhouse door?" she asked sharply. Silja had a habit of vacating places without looking back. She handed her one of the chipped, saucer-less Russian teacups from Viipuri and poured from the stainless-steel pot. Her hands shook so much that she had trouble aiming the coffee spout at the cup. "Keep it still!"

"I am!"

Taimi scrabbled in the half-empty sugar bowl for an unbroken cube to chase down her own cup of coffee, her third. She tucked the sugar between her tongue and bottom teeth, splashed a swallow of coffee onto the saucer, and tossed it into her mouth, swilling the coffee over the sugar cube. How many they would be again? Anneli and Heino, two; her first, Mervi and her weasel-husband, Iiro, four; she and Silja, six. Silja's brother was at summer camp and her cousins were taking summer English classes somewhere in England, the name of the town escaped her.

Silja sat cross-legged on the bench where Viktor used to

sleep, and where the scent of his pipe tobacco was still preserved in the corner of the room. She was making half-moon indentations in her slice of buttered rye. "Grandma, why do you keep those pictures in the outhouse?"

She meant Viktor's tattered pin-up girls, tacked on the rough walls, to spite her for their sleeping arrangements. "They were your grandfather's. You know that." What was Silja asking about those for, all of a sudden?

"But why do you still have them?" A shrewd look lit up her bright, young eyes.

Yes, why had she not taken down those pictures that continued to engage in a battle that had ended. Her own salvos—newspaper clippings of Bible verses—were also still pinned above her pillow, unread. Why then? Guilt, perhaps, a begrudging respect for his masculinity. Viktor had been a soldier, had saved them all from becoming Soviet citizens. Who was she to tell a war veteran he couldn't at least look at pretty women, when she herself…Or maybe it was to remind herself that he had wanted someone else besides her. That that's how life was—that she hadn't been his one and only.

"I guess I'm used to them," she said finally and saw that Silja wasn't satisfied. Maybe she already knew better, or Anneli had shared some of the family secrets with her. And maybe it was obvious to Silja that her grandfather had slept there, where she was sitting, and not next to his wife in the single cot in the alcove. Her lumpy soap dish of a bed, a woman-shaped indentation in the middle, couldn't accommodate two adults unless they were spooning. By the time the house was finished, their spooning days were over.

She downed the rest of her coffee and went to the slop bucket in the cabinet under the hotplate, dumped the coffee grounds, and in the same fluid motion pulled down her underpants and peed into the bucket. Some gas escaped.

Silja held the slice of bread in front of her mouth and smiled. "Puks," she said, quoting what she herself used to say when Silja was little and someone farted.

"Puks," she replied, treasuring the moment. She was collecting them, as if on a string, for when she might need them, in case she lived through one more winter.

—

"So Many Men, So Little Time," they sang together to the radio, shaking out the rug in the hallway and sweeping underneath it. Taimi had no idea what the lyrics meant—she didn't speak English but had learned by heart the sounds of the words of popular songs.

At the well Taimi dipped the cast-iron bucket into the clanging depths and poured the water into the pail propped between her knees. Once upon a time she had brought up whole bucketfuls in a single go, but now she had to haul the water up in halves and even that was becoming hard. Her bad leg ached. Last year, gathering kindling in the woods, she had tripped on a root and crash-landed on a hulk of deadwood. One of the bone-hard branch stumps had speared her left shin and lodged between what Heino had called her tibia and fibula. She shrugged without admitting that she had believed the lower leg to consist of a single large "leg bone." Repeated applications of plantain leaves on the festering wound had not worked their usual magic, and the infection had taken weeks to tame.

Soon she would not be able to come here. Time had moved on. Even now she only came in summer, May through sometime in September, when the days began to feel sad and her apartment in town less so. Standing knee-deep in the potato field on a rainy afternoon, digging up the last spuds before the freeze, her fingers stiff with cold, she would imagine the illuminated city streets, the reflections of shop lights on wet cobblestones, and the knowledge added an extra dreariness to the squelch of mud beneath her rubber boots. Had Viipuri not been lost, she reminded herself, she would have grown old in a city anyway, unaware of potato fields and country cottages. She had grown up a city girl.

But in the airiness of the July day, the city's smells and the sounds of her neighbors reverberating through the concrete prefab held no thrall. She did not miss their laughter and fights and televisions, or, on sleepless nights, the upstairs neighbor banging in his bathroom. *Making coffins* was a midnight conviction of hers that sounded unreasonable as soon as she uttered it out loud to Anneli, but at night she believed it firmly. Or the young female who romped around with a pair of enormous mixed-breed dogs— only a loose woman—possibly a prostitute—would have such big dogs. "The size of them," she cried out in the garden.

She shook her head. What now? She was at the well, beneath the maple, the red plastic bucket at her feet in the grass. What was she doing? Getting ready for the party.

Changed into her good dress she went to check the parlor, where Silja had finished dusting. With her forefinger she test-swiped the lacquered sideboard. Through the wood she could almost feel the lavender letter from America locked inside the sideboard, hidden behind stacks of old postcards.

She surveyed the round table—laid with her best tablecloth, the rose-colored china from Viipuri, the pinecone-cake under its plastic dome, the open-faced sandwiches, and the sweetbread she and Silja had made—and felt more than heard the rumble of an approaching car. It was the one with the loud sports engine that made the windows reverberate—Mervi and Iiro's car. The rumble became a roar, and as she hurried outside she remembered the day Viktor had ridden into the yard on his new Harley Davidson, bought with the last of the war subsidies without her knowledge. What a scamp.

More car doors slamming; Anneli and Heino's Fiat was also

there, and suddenly the yard was ringing with Anneli's laughter and Mervi's giggles. You wouldn't think they were women in their forties. Mervi, with a bouquet of carnations. Carnations! Probably grown in some foreign country. Iiro, self-conscious, tightly wound as always, and Anneli with a wrapped present under one arm and hugging Silja with the other, and Heino, staring at his shoes and smiling to himself. He and Silja embraced as well. All this hugging—who had started it? They had been apart for only a few days. There had never been any hugging in the family, and now suddenly they were all doing it.

"Happy birthday!" Mervi gave her the bouquet.

"Oh, that." She waved her hand but took the flowers. "The lilacs are in full bloom, you know."

Mervi went on smiling. She looked Silja up and down, taking in the white turtleneck and tight white jeans. "What a bombshell. Your mom told me you had changed."

Taimi humphed, knowing the reason for the turtleneck, and saw Iiro make a move toward Silja. But Silja slipped away and came to stand next to her. Good instincts, she thought and patted Silja's arm.

"How's life in Yankeeland?" Iiro rocked on his heels in front of Silja, wearing that stupid, toothy grin he didn't seem to be able to drop.

"A bit more civilized than here, looks like," Silja said, smiling sweetly.

"Life is the same wherever it is," Taimi said, deadpan, but wanted to laugh. Silja's sarcasm was new.

"Right, nothing special, just hanging out with your friends Elvis and Jane Fonda," Iiro said, pronouncing Jane in Finnish, *yahne.*

Would they never stop talking about America? She couldn't stand it, had to literally turn her cheek whenever one of them mentioned Texas, or the Cadillac Anneli and Heino had bought, or any of it really.

Anneli gave her the expensive-looking gift box from Stihlman's department store, probably some article of clothing. They were always buying her more things even though she never used what they gave her and had for years been storing their presents in the bedroom closet. When she died they would find all the gifts pristine, in their original boxes, the givers' names written on the packages. They could use the dresses and robes and unsuitable pajamas themselves.

In the parlor, Silja retreated to the far end of the sofa with her journal, and Anneli and Mervi and Heino took up the rest of the sofa. That left Iiro in the chair she had placed next to her own armchair. At least she wouldn't have to look at him.

"Yankeedoodle, are you writing in American to your American boyfriend?" Iiro asked Silja across the table.

Silja's cheeks reddened but she didn't look up. Heino rested his chin in his palm and regarded Iiro as though he were an interesting specimen under the microscope.

"Leave her alone, Iiro," Mervi said.

Iiro laughed. "I'll leave you alone."

The way people were getting divorced these days, she wondered why Mervi and Iiro didn't. He had next to nothing useful to say. His usual target of ridicule was Mervi, "my lizard companion," he called her. Early on she had stood up for her daughter, who suffered from eczema, but eventually they all got used to tuning him out. His nastiness became woven into the family fabric, like a colicky child, or a phlegmy cough in the back room.

"How's your leg, mom?" Mervi asked.

"Better a hole in the leg than in the bucket," she said and got up as if to prove the point. She served the second round of coffee from the pot under the warmer and imagined how she looked to them now, her spine bent, her hands trembling.

"Mom, what happened to your rings?"

Mervi again. She was one of those people who asked questions instead of offering insights. "In the kitchen. They get tight when it's warm." She had always lied easily about small things. They all stared. "I may just keep them off, for the summer," she went on, unable to stop. "Like a summer widow."

Silja laughed out loud. 'Summer widow' was the term the tabloids used about people who spent part of their vacation alone because their spouse was away, and the implication was that they would or at least could have an affair. She and Silja had read the article out loud together in the paper Silja brought from the airplane.

"Where do I sign up for that?" Mervi asked.

"Don't be an ass," she told her daughter, and immediately wished she could take it back.

Iiro laughed, and his eyes traveled across his sister-in-law's chest. Anneli's bosom was visible to all the world in a scoop-necked, tight-fitting t-shirt. It was obvious where Silja was getting her influences. Taimi kept her lips pinched, making sure the words didn't escape this time.

"So your boyfriend's a cowboy?" Iiro returned his attention from mother to daughter, his foot tapping nervously.

"There's time enough for boyfriends," Taimi said.

"Better to have lots of boyfriends so she doesn't marry the first one, like some of us," Mervi said.

Again Taimi clamped her mouth shut, the upper and lower false teeth snapping together. What a thing to say. It was true though—she, Mervi and Anneli had all married their first man. "Not everyone has to get married," she finally said, surprising even herself.

Silja stopped writing and Heino got up to examine the cereus.

"*Some* people never did…" Iiro looked around for someone to aim his grin at.

"Bracteole," Heino said from the window, without turning around. "*Brak-tee-owl*," he enunciated again and poked at a bud.

What was Heino talking about—was he trying to run interference, to stop Iiro's insinuations? She wanted to tell him not to touch the plant, but they weren't on speaking terms. "Viktor was a good man," she said to the room. "He fought for this country." She took the porcelain creamer, next to the matching sugar bowl.

In the kitchen she waited to refill the creamer until her hands stopped shaking. The once-fat, work-whittled wedding band lay on the shelf, and next to it, the thin engagement ring with its disappearing engraving. Only a ghost of their two names and today's date, sixty years earlier. When they used to argue, Viktor would sometimes shout, "Damnit, I should have moved to America with Lilja!" The girls had heard him say it many times, and who knew if Viktor had told them other things on his death bed. *Some people never did...*if Iiro knew, they would all know. She would put a stop to it.

—

Afterwards as they tidied up, Silja chattered about the boy in Texas and the things they did together—rodeos and roller-skating and driving to movies in the boy's older brother's car. Taimi had seen that kind of thing on television, on shows like *Happy Days*, where people watched movies from their cars, in big dark parking lots. She would talk to Anneli about letting a teenage boy drive her granddaughter around in a car, where they were free to do whatever.

The parlor had returned to its usual peaceful state. A faint aroma of mildew in the cool air blended with the fading smells of the summer day. Dressed in her long cotton nightgown, Taimi crouched to build a fire in the tile stove, to warm the room and hasten the flowering of the cereus. There would be no electric light tonight; artificial light might disrupt the blooming. She had even turned off the television after the eight-thirty news. Since then, Silja had been curled up under the red quilt, writing in her journal. The quilt had belonged to Taimi's grandmother, who had bequeathed it to Taimi's mother, upon whose death she had inherited it. It was her nicest one but it made her uneasy—as though it might still harbor her dead mother's skin cells. Maybe she would leave the quilt to Silja instead of one of her daughters—skip a generation.

Candle ends from the previous Christmas sputtered on the table, as the flames caught the dust of the ensuing year. Outside, the garden was being swallowed by dusk, but she could still see the outlines of the apple trees Viktor planted after the war—the translucent Astrakhan wonder apples with their reptilian scars and see-through flesh had been her favorite in Viipuri. He had gone back during a lull in Finland's war with Russia and brought branches of the Astrakhan, and grafted them onto the young trees around the cottage. They had both been so strong then; she had rowed the boat across the sound to catch the bus into town, ridden instead of walked her bike to the village grocery, warmed the sauna, collected firewood, grown cabbages and vegetables, picked and preserved apples, strawberries…Viktor died in this room, on the same pullout where Silja now lay, her head on the same pillow as Viktor's had been when he asked Taimi to get him a beer to help with the pain, asked and asked, on that day and in days previous, but she would not make an exception. *You should have given him the beer*, Heino said to her afterwards, and she had never spoken to him again.

Her breast ached with a pain she would have described as shrill if anyone had asked, but she was not going to tell anyone. With Ester gone there was no one left who was her equal, no one with whom to share a private worry or spin a yarn about Viipuri. No one living for whom she was just "Taimi." She knew it was cancer. Everyone on her side of the family had died of it, and she was ready—her main life events had all happened in uneven years, from birth to marriage. She certainly wasn't going to a doctor, had been to one only once, to the man who had gone inside her to find the hole in her gut. It hadn't made a difference. The hole and the burn in her stomach remained to this day.

She checked the cereus—not yet—and moved the armchair closer to the crackling fire. From the sideboard she pulled out the leather-bound album that documented her first years of marriage to Viktor—the wedding, the births, the christenings. A long sigh rose in her chest, like the wind before rain. She lifted her feet in their double woolen socks onto the basket of firewood and unpinned her long braid, the end of it a silverfish tail upon her breast. She turned the pages of the album, from the single photo of herself as an infant and a portrait of her parents, to pictures of her and Viktor interspersed with snapshots from his life before her and the children, as a handsome sailor who traveled the world on steamships and sailboats—so handsome that her friends had flirted with him, even Ester. But somehow he had chosen her, the most serious and chaste of them all. Here was Viktor leaning against a pole fence in summertime, behind him bales of hay scattered across a field, his smile suggestive, eyes playful—who had taken the photo? Who was he looking at with that expression? It wasn't her. She ripped out the photo. It came off easily, the glue pulverized by time.

The next page was taken up by a large black-and-white picture of Viktor hanging high up in the mast of a sailboat, dangling by one hand from a rope, his jaw tilted, the wind tousling his hair. She tore out the picture and snapped the stiff cardboard in half. On the back was the blue stamp of the photography studio and the date—June of the summer of Lilja Asp.

By the time she had found out about Viktor's brief relationship with Lilja, and about the pregnancy, she and Viktor were already engaged and had a date for the wedding. Lilja had left for America, before anyone could see the state of her.

Things like that befell women who didn't protect themselves. She glanced across the room at Silja who had fallen asleep over her journal. Had she too looked like that once—sensuous and ripe? Was that how Viktor had seen her? She plundered through the album, removing picture after picture from his premarital past, leaving only those in which he accompanied her or the children. As presidents did, she would control her legacy before the disease took her.

When she was done, a pale square remained where each photo had been, the vacant spaces captioned in her own sure cursive: "Viktor in Viipuri, 1937." "Viktor, first voyage." "Viktor in Monrepos Park." She examined her left hand, the pale band of skin protected by the missing rings for sixty years. Gone so fast. She reached for the stove latch and slid the photos into the embers. The cardboard caught slowly, and she watched the face of Viktor the sailor crumple to black in a frame of tiny flames.

With the key in her apron pocket she unlocked the sideboard and took out the lavender envelope addressed to both Viktor and her. The name in the return address belonged to a woman she didn't know but knew of. *Lily McAlister*, daughter of Lilja Asp. *New Jersey* said the return address, written in the hand of an American woman with Viktor's blood in her veins. The letter informed them of the death of Lily's mother, Lilja, at age eighty-two, and asked for permission to visit "my siblings" in Finland. The audacity—a complete stranger writing to *her* in bad Finnish, wanting to meet her "siblings." *Her* siblings!

She had considered replying to Lily McAlister but didn't know English, and her shaking hands only produced the wobbly stick-scrawl she used on birthday cards for the grandchildren. As so many other times, no answer was the best answer. She stuck fresh birch logs into the stove and stuck Lily McAlister's American envelope in between. The thin paper caught fire and vanished into a heap of powdery ash.

Outside, the door of the outhouse was slamming against the shed. The wind had picked up, it rushed through the garden in furious gusts, shaking branches and leaves. She saw a slight thinning of darkness already beyond the spruce and blinked in confusion, suspended between her memories and the task at hand. Then she remembered the cereus.

The mops from earlier in the day had opened into great white flowers. Tiny beads of dew glistened where the greenish stamens disappeared into the rich pink in their middle. Taimi prodded one of the stems gently. The flower seemed to disperse a kind of substance, the outer tepals reaching out long tendrils and emitting a scent, was it vanilla? yes, only more intoxicating. If only Ester were here to see this.

"Silja," she whispered, not wanting to break the spell. Silja woke up immediately and came to stand next to her. Shoulder to shoulder they gazed at the blooms, already wilting.

"Like a water lily," Silja said, cradling one of the three flowers between her palms. "I wish they lasted longer." She yawned and returned under the covers.

—

Taimi looked back briefly at her granddaughter asleep under the blood-red satin quilt.

She left her wool socks on the plastic doormat she'd crocheted herself—after she was gone they would find hundreds of the plastic milk bags from the 1960s, washed clean and stacked neatly in a cabinet, ready for cutting to strings and crocheting. She stepped into the restless night.

The cherry trees where the starlings had been were silent now, the black sphere behind them, the well. As she passed the maple, the tree rained upon her its seeds during a sudden wind gust. She continued past the strawberries and the old cabbage patch, toward the potato field, the grass beneath her calloused soles soft and cool—when last had she walked without her shoes on? Going down to the sound for a midnight swim with Ester, years ago, maybe.

She sat down next to the potato field, between the lilacs and the shit tree. This was where she and Silja used to spread their blanket on hot summer days, telling stories and shelling peas and singing Tirlittan in the shit tree's shade. *Tirlittan kiipes puuhun, Tirlittan putosi, Tirlittan kuoli ja kuopattiin*…Above her, branches twisted and heaved.

She placed her feet in the outermost groove of the potato field, her heels snug against the bottom. Her land.

In the atlas, Taimi had located the state of New Jersey and found to her satisfaction that it was thousands of kilometers from Texas, in a different corner of the swollen expanse of America.

Her children might know that there had once been someone named Lilja in their father's life, but they didn't know about Lily McAlister, and now they never would.

She wet her hands in the dew and, since there was no one to see, pulled up the hem of her nightgown to feel the dew on the dry, wrinkled skin of her thighs. Her thighs that Viktor had loved and later forgotten, and later yet, left behind to walk alone in the rooms that he had built for the two of them and their girls.

She wrapped her arms around her shoulders and lifted her chin up to the wind, rocking her body side to side. In the back of her head, somewhere behind her, she heard the church bells that had tolled at Viktor's funeral nearly thirty years ago—the slow, ponderous death knell—gong……each strike trailed by a low, metallic scream, as if by the spirit of mourning trapped inside the bell, each strike a notch closer to eternity, and lingering so long that it was as if it had lasted until this very moment in a potato field in Southern Finland, in the odd year of 1993.

VIRGINIA BEACH

IN THE PHOTO, YEARS LATER: the face of the father, the rest of him covered in sand, and a toss of waves in the background. The blur in the foreground: the rise of the mother's hip in a pink bikini as she lay on her side to catch the sun.

They were new immigrants and had found the beach on a Virginia tourist map, and as with all of their family fieldtrips during that first American year, had left D.C. early to beat the weekend traffic.

It was a perfect beach day—only a few skinny clouds decorated the blue sky over the Atlantic—and the parking lot was full when they entered through the gate.

The parents unpacked while the boy, five, and the girl, ten, blew air into their inflatable beach toys in the backseat. His was a lifesaver with a dragon head, hers a blue raft.

When the toys were squeaky-stiff, the children took off toward the waves, glinting behind the wooded picnic area.

You know that feeling—the long pine needles under your bare feet in the cool sand, and the way the sand becomes scalding as soon as you're out of the shade.

They ran full tilt all the way to the water and stopped to take it all in. Back home in Finland, there was a shoreline, sure, but nothing like these crashing waves, and they rushed in, screaming over the mother's warnings. They turned, knee-deep in the surf, and saw her lips moving, but couldn't hear her in the din of the blue wall that was approaching, gathering strength, booming ashore and nearly knocking the two of them down.

When the water began to recede and gouged the sand from beneath their feet, the corners of the little boy's mouth turned down, and he pinched his sister's thigh with his sharp little nails as the wave seemed to suck them seaward.

She could see, as they stood in the bubbling expanse of sand, that they hadn't moved at all and that another tall wave was coming at them, foaming at the crest.

The beach was full—families, children, couples sprawled out on towels and sitting in sunchairs underneath umbrellas. In the middle of it all, the pale-skinned parents were setting up for an all-day picnic.

When the children returned from the water, they set to burying their father in the sand, pretending he was helpless and in their power, and they didn't notice right away that some of the other beachgoers were casting looks at them.

The girl eventually noted two brown-skinned boys sitting next to their mother on a towel, a few dozen feet away, both boys gazing at her and her family with a serious expression that she didn't recognize—but there was curiosity in it. What are you looking at, she thought, and stared back at them, trying to see her family through the eyes of an American: four people with blond hair, with a little boy who was running around naked.

She investigated her surroundings. All the other children had swimsuits, even the babies. The men wore swim trunks, with ample coverage compared to her father's scant European briefs. And though her mother wasn't the only one in a two-piece suit, her string bikini showed *a lot*.

She felt the wall of silence that surrounded them. They had become an island.

They ate their lunch in the middle of the silence. The parents conferred in whispers. As soon as they had eaten, they began to pack up, slowly and furtively.

The girl didn't understand it but believed they had committed some sort of wrong, maybe even a crime—but whether the wrong had to do with being there or in leaving, she wasn't sure.

In the car, the mother searched for another beach on the map while the father tried to exit via the entrance, to avoid paying the recreation fee—"We weren't here very long," he said and drove straight into the spike strip hidden in the asphalt. The girl sank down in the backseat as her father reversed, red-faced, and circled round to the attendant's booth to pay.

"Why do we have to go," the boy asked in loud English. No one answered.

Back on the anonymous freeway, they wondered what sorts of people would be on the next beach, in the next parking lot. What would they look like in those people's eyes? Would they be welcome there?

And what were they anyway, the girl asked, but only to herself. Finnish, European, white? Were they all different—all people—and if so, why didn't anyone say it? She felt cheated.

In America, it seemed that you were always facing yet another enormous wall of something inexplicable, coming at you out of nowhere, washing away the ground under your feet.

You know that feeling—of being reminded, again, and then again, that you are powerless.

STETSON GIRL

1

ME TULIMME MERESTÄ, we came from the sea. The first woman crashed through the waves and slapped onto the sand like a flounder.

Brighton Beach, low tide. The sun has fried white crêpe edges in the sand from the foam of departed waves. Under a filmy day-time cataract of moon, the winds from an impending storm whisk bits of straw and dried seaweed into the air. Speeding insects collide with my bare legs—besides me, only old Russian and Ukrainian men are out today, speed-walking in tiny swim briefs, chins upturned and noses held high into the bracing wind.

I wade into the water past an enormous gull dismembering a crab. The gull jerks the hard shell from side to side, like a cat with a herring, trying to pry loose the meat and casting suspicious glances at me over its gull-shoulder. I wade in further, as far as I can without wetting my shorts. In mid-June, the water is still cool.

I have just received Saari's annual birthday card in the mail. She started sending them after she left New York fifteen years ago. She sends them not on my birthday but on hers, June 10th. There is never any message, just 'Saari'—her name a proclamation of her importance—and no return address. The postmark though, dated on her birthday, is from *KAUPUNGINSAIRAALA TURKU*

ÅBO FINLAND. The long word means 'municipal hospital,' Åbo is Swedish for Turku, and Turku is the town in Finland where she became institutionalized.

I picture her in the hospital in the watery light of Nordic midsummer, medicated, compliant, dreaming of chickens.

'FINLAND,' the card says on the front in shiny, raised golden letters across a faded color photograph of three naked women in a sauna, each holding a bunch of birch twigs to cover her critical regions, as the Finnish expression goes. The cards are not actual birthday cards, but generic tourist highlights of local landmarks—the Functionalist railway station, a lively view of the market square in summer, the harbor with its medieval castle. Sometimes it's a real bottom-of-the-barrel card, like this remnant from the seventies. I don't know where she finds them. I don't even know if she's a patient or only drops the card in the hospital mailbox on her way somewhere. She was odd like that.

I rip the card into squares and let the wind pick them off my palm. I have come to anticipate these missives, but each time one arrives it brings a dismaying reminder of the past, and of the fact that my connection to my country of origin is so tenuous as to consist of a yearly postcard from a Finnish mental institution.

The waves retreat and the sea sucks the sand beneath my feet, and where moments ago waves splattered and swirled, there is now pristine, freshly filleted sand. I turn to shore, thinking of the words I once said to Meri here, on this beach—*me tulimme merestä*—we came from the sea. It was a joking reference simultaneously to our immigrant and our evolutionary pasts, and in my head, also a play on words that I didn't share with her; in Finnish, Meri means "the sea," and in the heat of our new love, I reveled in the convergence of her name and the seaside setting.

Saari is, literally, an island.

Saari = Joka puolelta veden ympäröimä (mannerta pienempi)

maa-alue. A land area (smaller than a continent) surrounded by water on all sides.

A thing that cleaves water. The opposite of water.

Synonyms: *shank, isle, islet, cannon.*

That year when Meri came to visit me in New York, I hadn't thought about her in a long time. She was attending a conference, and I had no idea that a year later she would be living in my apartment and that I was about to meet another Finn, Saari—two Finns for the price of one.

Meri and I had been childhood friends in Finland, very different, and had always liked each other exactly for that reason. We were also the losers of our middle school, shy and awkward and lacking confidence, she even more awkward than I. My single salvation was that I had once been to America, to New York, and had seen the Empire State Building. No one else had, and therefore didn't know what it was that I knew and they didn't.

At thirteen, Meri began to play ice hockey and I started cutting pictures of women out of magazines, making collages and dreaming short-term dreams of such and such distant, unknown boy. I sometimes shunned her for the company of more popular girls, girls who gave me the social cachet I didn't have and brought me closer to the boys whose sidelong glances I described in my diary in such detail that the left cuticle of my right middle finger thinned out from holding the pen every day for so many years.

Meri in eighth grade, in a white bra in the girls' locker room; I recall no other bras. Meri, unfazed by the boys and watching all through middle school as I approached one daydream-boy after another and stood in front of him and froze, unable to utter a word or make a gesture of interest—just stood there, waiting for him to take the initiative.

Before ninth grade my family emigrated to America, to the Midwest. Meri wanted to know everything about it, and I told her in my letters, painting it all in technicolor. She shared my fascination with America, the mystery, the allure. Maybe that's where her dream of living in America began, or maybe she already had it and I fed the flames, but I think I came to represent it—something almost unattainable, titillating and foreign, that could alter you and make you new.

A decade later, there she was, in the kitchen of my East Village apartment: Meri, through a vodka haze, in her twenties now, crawling toward me across the linoleum floor. Our reality shifted that very first night, and after dinner and drinks, the two of us were already lamenting that friendship so rarely manifested itself physically, and embracing, and a minute later kissing—praising each other: what a good kisser you are!

Who was this tantalizing beast, who, like me, had been bullied at school but was now pushing me against the sink, and whom I was kissing back in a way that I'd never kissed anyone?

But she was married, and my passion was still at a slight remove, like a shadow or a hallucination. Cruel in my ignorance, I was only about to learn what it costs to want someone so your insides burn. I jumped down from the sink where she had put me and ordered her out of my apartment, back to her hotel. Her hunger shocked me, I didn't understand what it was. I had never seen anything so huge and at the same time so helpless.

Each day of her week-long visit, at the last moment of retreat, I shut the gates and left her standing behind my door, writhing with want. Until the last night.

It was unseasonably warm, the August sun a smoldering slice of red, cocky and dangerous. People bared their winter skin and passing cars with rolled-down windows hurled snippets of song over the pedestrians. Meri and I followed canned music from a side street to a festival banner and multicolored paper lanterns swaying in the night wind. At the end of the block, a Ferris wheel with yellow light bulbs arranged in carnival patterns rose and fell, implausible in the narrow canyon of tenement buildings.

Around the world for $1. Her visit nearly over, we held hands and looked into each other's eyes, not letting go as we swung, strapped into the metal carriage high above the rooftops, and we fell, fell…It wasn't until that night that we made love, deliberately and with our eyes open, in the crimson glow of my desk lamp, Chinese pop songs tinkling on the radio.

The plates had shifted. I couldn't get her out of my mind. It took me months to go after her, to Finland, even though I had to fabricate a family emergency to take a leave from my job as foreign-student advisor at the technical college where I still work. I went, even though Meri still lived with her husband, even though she emailed to tell me she had also already taken on a lover.

But nothing is entirely true until you test-drive it at home.

Not even love. Especially love. And my love was still rooted in Finland.

I sublet my apartment exchange for my grey, slushy hometown, arriving to show Meri that I was *real*, meat and bones, not a figment of some big-city interlude—I was something she couldn't *live* without. But in that watery light, the heat and charge of New York were missing. One day, taking a walk together, high on a rocky ledge in the woods, she tried to get me to yell out at the rock wall opposite us to sound an echo. Let go, she was trying to say and went first, and the echo answered in a handsome boom. All I could produce was a cough.

Afterwards, I walked her to the bus stop, and it was my desire for her that was deafening. "You are the woman of my life!" I breathed and kissed her, hot, rough, abrupt, through the steam of our breath rising in the chill.

She said nothing, but energy like that leaves a mark, it can't be ignored.

I hid behind the curtain in the kitchen of my temporary

rental, still in my coat, and watched her pace back and forth under the bus shelter. Why under it? It wasn't even raining. She glanced up at my window once in a while, but I'm sure she didn't see me, her glasses fogged up in the cold. I thought: there you are, and I will never be rid of you.

I kept up my campaign. "We'll never have a chance like this again. No one else can be what we are for each other." The smell of cardamom coffee wafted in the student union. Cigarette smoke and giggling, The Doors on the jukebox.

"Yes. But. It would almost be like incest. We're too close," she said quietly.

"Incest! We're friends. And you're the one who chased me across the floor in New York! If you want to experience something amazing in this life, you have to be brave. You have to break some boundaries. Be afraid, sure, but then be brave!"

She looked small and fearful, nothing like the woman-beast who had lifted me onto the kitchen sink.

"Am I going to have to get down on my knees?"

"Jesus Christ—"

The café was closing. It was Sunday afternoon and the wind outside fierce, and as we stepped out onto the sidewalk, a strong blast ravaged a pile of leaves and garbage left over from the seasons before snow and sent them scattering across the street, up the hill toward the Municipal Hospital.

Climbing the hill I was so full of certainty that I thought I might faint. "Seriously, I'll go down on my knees."

A little smile flickered in the corners of her mouth. Behind the tall hospital fence, an emergency helicopter lifted off. It swiveled in place, rose higher, and sent candy wrappers and more dry leaves flying into our faces. We looked at each other. Meri's short hair stuck up off her forehead and she crinkled her eyes behind dusty lenses. I was ready. A hum raged in my ears, blood pounded though my veins. Life was here and it was now.

As an adult you rarely feel that kind of joy, over the fact that everything is possible—because *this* is possible, and I would do what I had to, to achieve it. I will never again be as strong as in that moment.

I grasped her arms.

"Please." She tried to stop me from sinking down to my knees.

We parted, late. I hurtled home on my bicycle, the sky above full of stars, and I was gazing at them when my front wheel hit a boulder in the road and life gave me the middle finger and I broke my own, catapulting over the handlebars into a mess of weeds and brambles. I tore open my left knee and had to walk the bike home the rest of the way, the chain rasping and the back-wheel squawking. Blood seeped through my jeans and the earphones of my Walkman remained where they had turned ninety degrees during the crash—on my face and the back of my head. I didn't notice them until I saw myself in the bathroom mirror.

There is still an L-shaped scar on my left knee that prickles and burns whenever the weather turns. "L for lesbian," I used to think. Or "love."

Saari fingered it once when she was drunk and asked me how I had gotten it.

"From falling head over heels," I told her and removed her hand.

2

MERI'S HAND GLIDING ACROSS MY BARE BACK, in July, in New York, where I had finally managed to snare her with a job teaching English to foreign students at my own college.

I hadn't missed Finland before, but now I saw it in everything and spent rich moments admiring the solitary hair sprouting from the silky skin of her right breast, like a midget birch in the Arctic. When she is old and wrinkled, I thought, this steely chest hair will still shoot forth as valiantly as now.

We continued where we had left off, in the collective caress of the July breeze, on the sticky sidewalks, meandering past the gay men and their erect nipples in Chelsea, whiling away weekend afternoons in dusty bars, drinking slowly, kissing under the light of neon beer signs, recoiling and merging like eels against each other. A time as close to childhood as it's possible to have as an adult, our steps firm and full of purpose, though we had no idea where our feet would land next, or whether they would land at all. As a child, that kind of lightness follows you everywhere. There are no miracles, only life. It never occurred to me to be afraid.

We had ripped open each other's floodgates, and the past gushed out: the music of our youth, our mother tongue, the other tongue, old jokes, first loves, original friendships, Finland, America, all tumbling out full of significance and life. But it wasn't only that we had a second chance at childhood, it was "twice the first time"—everything was doubled: love, sex, words.

Finally, the life around me reflected the landscape within me.

But in detonating the fragments of Finland that I had stored in my tiny immigrant's pillbox, she cast into relief my smallness in the immensity of America. She reminded me that, here, where I didn't belong, everything began and ended with me—I had no family or safety net, no one to pick me up if I fell. I was a spore airborne in a great big world.

Together, we could safely float on the wide-open sea between our two continents. We were free, we were new people. The things we had been bullied for—ice hockey, nerdiness, shyness, silence—were now things other people prized. Our shared experience of being social outcasts and emerging from that past to America, and rediscovering one another in New York, brought us closer together the same way our outsidership once did as teenagers.

As then, it bred distrust. We knew how much we were each willing to sacrifice to survive.

I took her to Brighton Beach.

The water was fuzzy that day, the way it is at the end of summer, full of plant and human detritus. Trash floated around me as I swam, circling the spot where Meri stood waist deep in water and gazing into the horizon, lost in thought. I opened my eyes underwater. Her olive skin glowed white and her torso was cut off in the middle, her head and breasts visible only as a reverberating mass caught on the water's surface. When I came up for air, she was olive and delicious again, and I was flooded with such lust that I began to splash toward her, heart thudding, and leapt into her arms laughing and crying, and she caught me, surprised, and threw me back into the sea—as you would a sack of grain from a truck-bed.

Afterwards we sat in a boardwalk restaurant drinking Russian vodka and sampling pickled herring. She placed a thin stack of postcards on the table.

"Who are those for," I asked.

"Mother, of course. And Dennis."

Of course.

She had left husband and lover, she'd said, and though alarm bells sang in my head, I had agreed to let her move into my apartment. The ex-husband was everywhere, his handwriting in her books in inscriptions promising "everlasting, deepest love," his phone calls from Finland coming at all hours, prompting her to carry the phone into the kitchen and close the door behind her. I asked if she planned to keep talking to him so often and saw a glaze slide over her eyes.

In the beginning, I had been the bigger one, the powerful one—we were still on my turf. By late August, at a restaurant with her new queer teaching colleagues, she made a joke about the dresses I sometimes wore. Suddenly she was the one with cachet, and she wielded her power. She told us how she had acquired her temporary Finnish lover at a gay bar in Finland after her New York trip and referred to the young woman as a 'pocket dyke'—something so young and small as to fit in a pocket. "I was her first," she said and winked at me across the table as-if conspiratorially; we had both been each other's "first." I thought about how, at home, she was too scared to call the gas company but kept it to myself.

"Ahh, the tender meat of fresh chicks," her colleague said. "You broke her heart?"

"The heartbreak of losing your first woman—there's no other like it, I've heard."

That'll never happen, I thought as I joined the others in knowing laughter.

Our love was big, it was continental. Still I kept trying to amplify it, reveling in imaginings of something terrible happening, so I could save her. What if someone broke into our apartment and did something to her? Or attacked her in the street and called her a homo? In these terror scenarios I arrived just in time to rescue her, punch the criminal in the face. I had never hit anyone, but I was ready.

Beneath this fever was a gaping absence, and a pretense that we weren't who we really were, but an American version of ourselves, new and improved.

Warning signs were everywhere. We ate pot brownies and had the kind of sex I had always dreamed of, but afterwards she told me as we lay on the bed that even though I probably thought that my eyes were closed, they were actually open a crack, and showed a slice of white eyeball. She laughed, I laughed—at how the whole time, instead of looking scintillatingly sensual against the pillows, eyes closed and lips parted, I had actually looked comical.

I looked into her eyes and let my love flow forth, but almost without fail she'd seem a little surprised, uttering a nervous joke, a harsh comment, a cold flash of something. I waited for the moment of understanding to flood her face. I lived for the moment when the hard sheen in her eyes would melt away; I was certain that once she reached understanding, she would reach me.

In the best of times I felt like this: Standing in a swamp up to my shins I am gazing upon a limitless spread of soft, velvety moss, all peace and birdsong. In the worst of times: I open the door outside and the sky dumps a suitcase of snow down my neck. Cold, wet and surprised.

3

ON THE WAY HOME FROM BRIGHTON BEACH, the F train stops mid-track, in an urban copse of honey locusts. The coming storm has the air dripping with moisture, and a whiff of something at once floral and dank reaches in through the ventilation window. Maybe it already smelled like this twelve thousand years ago, before subways and elevated tracks traversed the creek beds and rivers, and mastodons trudged from Brooklyn to Manhattan gobbling the red pods of honey locusts into their hairy maws. They gnawed the bark off the branches, so the tree developed sturdy thorns to fend off the feeders.

I've always liked the story of the thorns—the mastodons are gone, but the thorns remain. They came about in the course of millennia but we only have this one lifetime to evolve in one direction or another, grow thorns or shed them.

On the walk home from the subway, plastic bags sail through the air, white, black silver-striped from the liquor store, yellow from the grocery, rustling and flapping as they pass overhead, some soaring above the rooftops. I wait for the storm inside, and finally it does. The wind vanishes. Then, the first lighting strikes and blanches the soot-black sky, and the reeds and shrubs in the empty lot across the street come alive. Lightning flash like disco lights and I count seconds in 300-meter increments, the way we were taught as schoolchildren in Finland, one-two-three, one-two, one. I lose count as the wind returns, it seems to blow straight out of the earth, through last year's leaves and weeds, through hollows in the asphalt, with such force that anything that can, moves.

There is a thud, followed by a crash coinciding with a yowl, from the apartment downstairs. I have never heard a cat land like that.

"Get your fucking whore's ass out of here," my landlady, Mrs. Belvedere, screams.

"Fuck you. You can't tell me what to do you old cunt," replies a younger voice, her granddaughter's.

"Don't talk like that to your grandmother!" a man roars.

"Fuck you, Charlie. *Dad.*"

There is snarl from the old lady and another crash, this time with shattering glass.

"Goddamn fucking shit I can't take this," the girl screams and makes for the door, for in a couple of seconds it slams and her steps recede down the hallway.

After a few minutes there is a shuffling sound. The cat begins to meow. Something hits the door and the cat shuts up. I've called the City to get them to interfere, but no one ever comes. This is not the America I knew or Meri imagined as teenagers. Next to this, our three-way melodrama was mere shadow play in a New York City alleyway—and of the three of us, only Saari achieved her fifteen minutes of American fame.

As an immigrant, you often feel crazy—or that everyone else is crazy—and in the end, it seems purely arbitrary that it was Saari who ended up at the mental hospital in Turku—it could have been any one of us.

There is a flash in the curtain, a white cat darting up the fire escape. Then, great ice-blue eyes in a rhombus of the metal security gate. It's Belvedere's skittish cat—long, lean legs and a face shaped like an arrowhead. It stares right at me, in the lashing rain. I sit down in front of the gate, staring into those eyes. The moment stretches and I know I will lose in this game. She knows as well and begins to meow, without pause, finally nearly yelling and never letting go of my eyes.

I open the lock on the security gate. The screech of steel raises the hairs on my arms and though it's warm and muggy I feel a chill.

The cat bounds in as if it lived here. I retreat to the kitchen. It follows me, hollering. Stops then, about three feet from me, demanding.

This cat knows what it wants. The most perfect, harmonious and satisfying sensation I have ever experienced—the hot froth of steaming milk foams, swells, climbs up my sides; like a heart surging toward another.

My heart, though, breaks now, because I would like to be good to this cat and save it from the Belvederes, but I am allergic to cats and I have to chase her out. I don't know what got into me in the first place, why I even let her in. I pick her up and put her in the hallway.

4

With Meri, almost immediately and without knowing it, I began to look for a buffer, something to displace my love for her— divert it so that it wouldn't notice how badly it had been betrayed.

At the start of the fall semester Meri and I met Saari at the foreign-student orientation. I was onstage with my supervisor getting ready for our presentation, when she nudged me and indicated a tall woman in a Stetson hat jammed down low on her forehead. "That one. The Stetson girl. PhD in animal neurology. Keep an eye on her."

"Why?"

My supervisor smiled with her white teeth. "Some people need more than others." Whatever she may have known about Saari, she never shared with me.

Throughout my supervisor's presentation, from my seat at the back of the stage, I saw the woman in the cowboy hat glancing in my direction every now and then. As always, I was nervous about introducing myself to the crowd of students, so as to be recognizable to them on campus.

After my brief comments, as everyone was filing out for the after-party, the woman in the Stetson remained seated. Since I'd have to pass her on my way out, I thought I might as well pre-emptively introduce myself to this "problem student."

Even though she had been staring at me all that time, as soon as I walked up to her, she looked away. Her name tag said 'Saari Halonen'—a Finnish name. "Wait—you're Finnish," I said, in Finnish.

She tilted her head to one side and looked me straight in the eye and said, also in Finnish: "Americans are made of paper." Then, she gave me a big, unwavering grin.

I gave her the benefit of the doubt—the judgments made by fresh immigrants in the early stages of immigration can be as harsh as the judgments of those who oppose their presence here. "Are you coming to the after-party?" The office was piggybacking on a neighborhood block party on the riverfront. I had hired an all-female cover band to play American favorites from the decades, for the benefit of the international students, as well as to impress Meri.

Saari didn't respond, and her face had returned to the usual Finnish resting face, inward and sullen. That didn't faze me, it was how our stunted Cold War generation had been brought up to behave.

She walked with me to the party, a few blocks away on a dead-end street. She was what would be called "a big girl," over six feet and with an outline that was distinctly unfeminine, and an air simultaneously of arrogance and oppression—like a resentful cop, or a bossy cafeteria lady. As we walked, I saw the same swagger reflected in her gait: she strode, though she seemed constantly on the verge of tripping.

I forgot all about her as soon as Meri appeared amid the lights and the arc of Manhattan Bridge across the skyline. We snuck around the corner to kiss and smoke some pot she had scored from our neighbors Tony and Camden.

Later, swaying to the band's rendition of "Seasons in the Sun," I was gazing up at two balloons that had escaped into the darkening sky. One was Winnie the Pooh and the other Scooby-Doo, the two balloons rubbing up against each other as they rose and fell, twisting and shivering, conjoined, as though they were having sex. That's when I saw Saari near the stage, also looking up at the balloons. There was something very intense about the way she stared at them. She met my gaze, and I felt as though she had somehow known all along that I would be standing exactly where I was, looking at the balloons, and had made sure she would be there too.

She walked over as if we were old friends, but when I introduced her to Meri, ignored her completely. Meri raised her eyebrows at me and turned back to Tony and Camden.

At a loss as to what to do about the silent Finn, I spotted a carnival-style shooting range off to the side and asked if she would like to try shooting rubber ducks for a prize. She gave me a sly look, a kind of wink-wink, as if we were co-conspirators. I missed on each of my turns, but she hit the bull's eye right away and won a big blue teddy bear. I gave her a little American-type hug of celebration, in my capacity as cultural ambassador, but she kept her arms to her sides—it was like embracing a telephone pole.

She stayed with us the rest of that night, carrying the big blue teddy bear and speaking to no one, not even at our apartment in the East Village, where she followed us with Tony and Camden.

—

Until Meri moved in, we had only spoken English together, but I was keen to carve out an ever-greater space for Finland in my American life. By moving to New York, she had merged me, the immigrant, with the original girl, the pre-emigrant, and made herself the bridge between my two worlds. I began to demand that we start speaking Finnish. There was a reason why, after years of dating Americans, I had fallen in love with someone from my own culture. I thought Finnish would change our relationship into something "truer."

Meri, on the other hand, preferred inhabiting the new American version of herself. For her, speaking English was more exciting, like donning a cape under which anything at all was possible. She had been married to a foreigner, and in some ways was as dilutedly Finnish as I was.

I plagued her by addressing her in Finnish, and she nearly always replied in English and diverted us back to something current, immediate. Instead of using my Finnish name, she called me Chicka, a misappropriation of the 'chica' of our Puerto Rican neighbors. Maybe it was her way of putting me in my place, taking away the reality that she was with me.

Maybe she had to conquer me, to complete some perverse project that dated back to our school days, when she was bullied and forlorn, before she could return to her roots, altered and new.

Saari began to visit us regularly after the orientation party, sometimes several times a week. When I came home from work I'd find her on the stoop, waiting. I welcomed her presence because it forced the three of us to speak Finnish.

But Saari's entrance always immediately killed the conversation and laughter, and it was obvious that she and Meri disliked each other.

As far as I knew, Saari had no other friends, though apparently she did talk to her colleagues at the lab, because she sometimes relayed to me conversations she'd had with them, invariably depicting her American coworkers as the most ridiculous, vacuous human beings, and all foreigners as the "sane" ones. She made an exception for the Americans who were in her weekly two-step club. She told me, proudly, she was a lifetime member of the Helsinki Country & Western Society and was once their Teen Two-Step Champion.

I didn't believe her. "Show me."

She got up from the armchair and clattered and pivoted back and forth across our parquet floor, a towering figure in the tiny living room, in her Stetson. Otherwise, if Meri was there or we played Monopoly with Tony and Camden, Saari was a silent observer. "Would you like to play," Tony sometimes asked as we laid out the game board. Saari would crack her knuckles and pull her hat down further.

She only ever answered a direct question if someone asked about her work. "I study chicken brains," she would say. Then she would pause and add: "I kill a chicken every day." You could tell she liked saying it.

Leaning against Meri's legs as we played Monopoly, I could feel her agitation when Saari was present. Her annoyance gave me a thrill—it was a kind of unstated but justifiable payback for all the late-night transatlantic telephone conversations with her ex behind the kitchen door.

After Saari had come by a dozen times, I decided to surprise her at work, in the Nat-Sci Building, across the Quad from my office.

The building was carved through with gloomy, ponderous hallways. The doorway of her lab, at the end of a long corridor, was the only one that shone with fluorescent light and human presence.

Saari didn't seem at all surprised when I walked in. She was bent over a wire cage with the top open, attaching something to a chicken, the leads coming from a nearby gadget with lights and meters. Behind her was a small office with a glass wall. She had pinned up old-style movie posters of buxom women with ample cleavage and dark-haired men holding their supine bodies.

She looked up but didn't greet me, so I went to the long wall of chicken cages and poked my finger through the wire.

"That's Tony. He's one of the youngest. Watch out, he might peck."

"You give them names?" It didn't escape me that the chicken shared a name with my neighbor.

"It makes it easier to keep track."

Her demeanor seemed different—easier, more relaxed. "What do you do with them?"

"Study their brains. How they develop. Provide stimulation and test them afterwards. Dissect the brain."

"Dissect the brain? You really kill them? Yourself?" I went closer, to see.

"Mmm."

"How?"

She shrugged. "Electroshock." She made a zapping noise and motion.

Her breath smelled of mineral—iron or copper. I glanced back at Tony, the chicken. "Why do you do it?"

"What?"

Her face was guileless and open. I thought maybe that was why she tried to hide her face so often—she had no filter, her reactions were completely uncensored. "The chickens. Why do you do it?"

She zapped the chicken she had been "tracking" on the table, her eyes on a monitor, the recorder that had been going suddenly dead. She didn't answer. The chicken lay in a heap.

It was hardly an endearing, much less a seductive move, but she was behaving like someone trying to impress a lover.

She was so odd that it seemed safe to indulge in this strange friendship, and we began to spend more and more time together. I got to feel admired and wanted, and Saari got someone to be with. She didn't say much but listened as I talked, telling her about work, or the road trip across America Meri and I were planning. Often I caught her watching as I subconsciously stroked my leg while reading, or wound my hair around my finger. I didn't mind—in those moments her face was full of a kind of innocence, and I felt privileged to evoke that in her.

"Saari-this and Saari-that," Meri said in Finnish one night after Saari had left. "I'm sick of seeing her face in my living room every other night, and sick of your 'special relationship' with that crazy bitch." She suddenly looked quizzical. "What the hell is it that you see in her?"

She makes me feel important, that's what, I thought. It was Thursday—the day that Dennis always called.

5

BEING WITH SOMEONE FROM YOUR OWN COUNTRY, in a new country, you finally feel important, like you matter, like you're catching firmament. There is no doubt that Meri and I had picked each other, first as friends, then girlfriends, just so we wouldn't have to feel like outcasts in our own lives, and then, into this mix we threw transatlantic migration and a whole other person who didn't belong in the picture.

One weekend, Meri and I had just made love when I went to take a shower, and unbeknownst to me, she had let Saari into the apartment and told her to wait in the kitchen.

Our bedroom and living room were connected, whereas the kitchen and bathroom were accessed via a hallway. Opposite our bed was a wall mirror that afforded a partial view of the living room as well as the hallway. Lying in bed, Meri saw Saari tiptoe into the living room from the kitchen and sit down in the armchair, with a direct view into the bathroom. I had left the door ajar, so when I stepped out of the tub naked and reached for the towel, Saari saw all of me as I stood drying myself and singing. I didn't see her until I came out.

"Hi," she said, making no attempt to pretend she hadn't seen me.

I ducked into the bedroom and closed the door. "Why didn't you tell me she was here?"

"I wanted to see what she'd do," Meri said in her normal voice. "And you."

"*Shhh.*"

"She just walked in. She was grinning all the way through you singing 'Surabaya Johnny.'"

"You should have said something!"

She shrugged. "Tell her to leave."

"I can't just *tell* her to leave."

"So give her a fucking lap dance then. I'm done with this shit." Meri jumped out of bed, pulled on her clothes. "Seriously."

After she left I lay on the bed, crying, and it seemed like an eternity before Saari finally left. She stayed away for a few weeks, but after Meri traveled for a conference, Saari turned up in front of our house, sitting in a steel-blue Mercury with the window rolled open.

The way she stared ahead through the windshield, her Stetson pulled down low, the radio blaring and her elbow sticking out, it looked as though she were on a road trip.

"Are you coming or going?" I asked.

"No." She got out of the car and followed me inside.

She had bought the vehicle from a colleague and conducted the sale in front of our building, where the car stayed parked until the Sanitation Department plastered a notice on it.

"When are you going to take it home," I asked when I ran into her on campus.

She looked past me and grimaced.

That night I found her in the Mercury, trying to start the engine. The blue teddy bear sat in the passenger seat. I walked around and got in and shoved the bear in the back. Saari had stopped trying to start the car, and I pursued a hunch I'd had for some time. "How come you haven't taken it home?"

She turned her icy blue eyes on me.

"Answer! Why aren't you using it?" I could almost see her eyes shattering and the unreachable part of her seeping through. "Let's go for a drive."

"I'm busy right now."

"Busy doing what?"

"I have to...go to the bank."

"Well, then you can drop me off on the way."

She stared through the windshield and blew out a mineral-scented gust.

"You don't know how to drive, do you?"

She picked up an empty soda can from the drink holder—one of my Frescas—and crushed it in her hand and threw it out the window.

"Saari, why did you buy the fucking car if you can't drive?"

"I wanted to learn," she yelled, "so we could take a big American road trip together!"

The foreign students' end-of-semester party was on the day that Meri was returning from her conference, and I didn't expect to see her in the seminar room where we gathered over a bowl of punch made from lab ethanol and cranberry juice, getting wasted—even Saari. She displayed her two-stepping skills in front of me, performing a kind of semi-erotic western-style gyration, to which I responded, to lots of whooping. I smelled her coppery breath and wondered what it might be like to kiss that elemental mouth—maybe she would come to life, like a fairytale princess, if only someone loved her. Like I had.

"One of these days," Saari said, as people clapped to rhythm all around her, "I am going to kill you beautiful people." She kept grinning and kicking her feet, in cowboy boots, and I didn't know how she intended it, but I thought of the chickens named after people and wished Meri was with me instead.

Later at home, the suitcase of snow I had been waiting for finally came.

It wasn't a suitcase actually, but the lack of one.

Meri buzzed the doorbell after midnight—she had lost her keys, left them in Finland.

I could smell the ethanol on my breath as we exchanged a kiss. "Where's your luggage?"

In the kitchen, she told me she was leaving, moving back to Finland.

No, she hadn't found anyone else. I kept asking, and within minutes it emerged that, yes, she *had* found someone else.

Swaying with the liquor still in me I began to fill a Hefty bag with every symbol of our relationship that I could think of, from takeout menus and matchbooks from restaurants where we had

eaten together, to the fresh flowers I'd bought before her arrival—
welcome home, my love—and the special foods in the fridge I'd
purchased to pamper her.

I was falling, tilting, there was no bottom.

Pentecostals used to disseminate a little leaflet in the subway,
with a drawing of Manhattan sinking into primordial sludge. We
had always laughed about it, but without Meri, the image was
no longer funny. As she was receding, I felt myself becoming an
immigrant again, in the New York of before her; an immigrant in
a city of immigrants, unanchored.

"At least you'll have Saari," she said.

The next day, taking our final New York City walk together,
to the Chelsea piers, the city was still beautiful, ugly, full of noise,
but already it creaked in its joints and bobbed beneath me, built as
it was on a foundation of mud.

I sat on a concrete divider with my back to the Hudson while
Meri twirled about with her camera, snapping scenes for some
touristic collection.

"Hey, let me take one more picture of you."

"Why?"

"Come on."

I raised my tear-streaked face and looked into the camera,
and thought of the night before, our last night together.

She eternalized my pain. I will never understand why.

From Chelsea, Meri went into a cab and I went home,
where the answering machine blinked the way it did when I hadn't
listened to messages for a long time. The phone kept ringing, and I
finally picked up. It was Tony, telling me the news of Saari's arrest
for driving under the influence and posing a danger to the public.
Later, on the local news, I saw her steel-blue Mercury racing
through downtown Brooklyn, up Flatbush Avenue, where a TV
crew had been covering a campus protest when they and others
were knocked to the curb by the vehicle.

Shots of the Mercury swerving, of people running out of the way, the Mercury coming to a stop at the intersection of Tillary, and a closeup of Saari grinning behind the wheel like Jack Valance. As police dragged her out to handcuff her, her Stetson fell to the ground and the whole time she had the same grin on her face as on that first night when she said Americans were made of paper.

Charged and sentenced, she, too, returned to Finland. I was busy with my broken heart, so it made little impression on me. I never really thought of her until the cards started coming.

6

THE STORM IN BROOKLYN continues into the night, and in the middle of it I wake to the cry of a fox in the woods. When I open my eyes, there is no sign of a fox, nor woods, in the bedroom.

But there is something.

The window is open and the curtains are whipping in the wind. Why is it open, it wasn't when I went to bed. The rain is coming in, and in between the thrashing curtains I see an MTA bus stopped at the intersection, all lights on but no passengers, only a driver with a great protruding stomach, staring ahead through the windshield wipers, waiting for the light to change. The driver is only a few room-lengths from where I sit—naked! I realize—don't turn your head, please don't look, I chant and try to pull the cover over myself, but something is in the way.

It's the window, it's wet from the rain.

The storm has slammed the top pane of the left-hand window into the room, all the way to the bed, even though it's at least five feet inside the room. The lower pane lies flat on the rug in front of the window, and it's only then that I notice that it's raining on my bed and that the storm is *inside*, squealing in the corners of the room, and perhaps it *was* a fox that cried? I consult myself in the wall mirror between the two windows, I am naked in the orange glow of the streetlight and holding a rain-splattered window in my lap, and my mouth is open like an *O*, and I can hear something hitting the wall downstairs, and the wail of the cat, and the girl screaming.

And finally I hear my own howl, it's the squealing in the room, the *ur*-gene in me crying to be let out, into nature, to run with foxes, away from this square-walled room, away from doors, thresholds, down comforters, job security, and city buses without passengers that idle on street corners; I want to return to the source, to smell fertile cells—her cells—my blood homes to *her*.

How long will it take for the body to forget?

And what is the point of memory, if it can be suppressed?

The night before Meri leaves New York for good, I come home to find the apartment empty.

I go to sleep alone.

When I wake up, her hot breath is in my ear, her shorn hair prickling my cheek like a beard—that morning she had said something about going to the barber's. Her profile against the window looks foreign and harsh, like that of an army sergeant.

It's very dark and quiet, only the exhaust system of the restaurant below rattles the window gate. Meri presses against me, but there is a canyon between us. I lie on the bed like an exclamation point, mummified, toes to ceiling, arms tight against my sides, as a cat howls in the backyard. We listen to its wrenching, human-like roars, and Meri's hands go between my legs and she is talking now and I am turning to stone. Her hair stubble stabs my neck and face and it breaks my heart that she has cut off her silky hair to this military mold. She pushes closer and I breathe no, and then NO, many times, but she is past the point of caring or lost in a vision of her own, and she will not stop. She is paying me back for something, and I wish the door buzzer would ring, that someone, anyone, would interrupt us.

I have not wanted to recall her outline, the warmth of her beautiful body, the familiar voice. Only once in a while, early in the morning, after sounding the depths of the mind's sea for hours, her voice sometimes carries out of the darkness, *say yes YES*, the way she taught me to say to my body, in the beginning, and it is all this I remember each year when the Stetson Girl's card arrives.

BALLERINA DREAMS

SHE WAS FAT AND SHE KNEW IT. Standing in the doorway of the dance studio in a pale-blue tutu her parents had bought for the Fairy Dance lessons, she fingered the froth of fringe protruding from her hips. At home in front of the hallway mirror she had smiled at her reflection, but now it seemed all wrong. She was the only one in blue, they were all in pink. Her parents never got it right.

She hesitated at the edge of the room, the shy one. She shunned the other girls and they her, and Madame had assigned the only boy in the class as her dance partner. He was as timid as she and peed in his pants. This made her even more ridiculous—not him, but her, because he, by virtue of being a boy, and a ballet-dancing boy, was a hopeless case anyway, but that she, a girl, was not only shy and fat, but also had as her partner this pee-boy was the final straw for the skinny, gossiping ballerinas in the class.

But mostly it was that she was fatter than the other girls.

After five classes she stopped going.

Her parents continued dropping her off and walked her by the hand into the lobby of the old building and made sure that she started up the stairs to the studio.

But she continued past the third floor and loitered on the next landing, listening to the excited twitter of the other girls filing into class. At the ping of the first keys being struck, she tiptoed down into the dressing room and clambered up onto the wide windowsill, behind the heavy burgundy curtains. She sat gazing down at the cobblestoned market square below, full of people because it was Saturday morning, and she envied them and her parents, who were also down there shopping. Under her breath she sang *Oi niitä aikoja, oi niitä aikoja*—those were the days my friend, we thought they'd never end, her favorite song on the radio, repeating the refrain over and over because that was all she remembered.

On the clap of Madame's hands, preceding her announcement of the day's last exercise, she slipped out of her hiding place and crept downstairs to her parents, waiting in the little red Fiat. They waved to her, eager and pleased to be giving their child such a wonderful opportunity, the kind they themselves had never had.

A few Saturdays went like this. Then, one day, her parents were early and decided to come up to see her dance. She was behind the curtains when she heard her mother greeting Madame. The music ended and she imagined all the adults looking at each other in wonderment. "But where is she?" she heard her father asking. "You mean the shy, quiet girl?" Madame asked. "She hasn't been here for weeks. We thought you'd withdrawn her."

The three adults came into the dressing room, opening the doors of closets and bathrooms. Her father peeked behind the curtain.

"Oh my God," Madame said.

She climbed down from the windowsill to face the entire cast of scandalized, derisive little girls gathered behind Madame's hips, craning their necks to see her, even the pee-boy.

Her mother was furious. She was reinstated. Her mother demanded it. The following Saturday, she once again clasped the clammy hand and thin shoulder of the pee-boy. He had won a new confidence following her humiliation, so that now even he looked down on her. But he still peed in his pants, and she smelled the private, pungent smell of sodden cotton for the whole 45-minute class as they bent and pliéed in awkward misery.

Years later, already living in America, she ran into one of the "girls" at her local bank branch. The girl was a teller and still had the same bobbed haircut she had worn then. The woman recognized her immediately, exclaiming warmly, but she herself couldn't help thinking, look at you, and look at me, in America.

After that, whenever she imagined her old ballet classmates, she felt the warm glow of vindication as she permitted herself to picture their humdrum lives, their workaday clothes, their ballerina dreams long since lost.

COUNTRY FICTION

THE SERIOUS FINN WHO SAID LITTLE in company but a lot in private and cackled like a wanton hag wasn't the love of my life.

Yet even now, two decades later, when I look at the single photograph of her, something in me comes alive again. I prop up the picture on my desk, between the radio and the pot with the wax flower plant. The plant is an offshoot of the one my grandmother brought from Viipuri in 1944, before the Russians stole her city. On a visit back to Finland, I snipped off two leaves from the sinewy vines, which had taken over my parents' dining room since my grandmother's death. I stashed the leaves within the pages of volume two of Väinö Linna's epic *Under the North Star*, the trilogy of the Finnish civil war. On the plane, I checked "No" in response to the Customs Declaration Form's question of whether I was bringing live plants or agricultural products to the United States. In Finnish, the word for "leaf" applies both to the leaves of books as well as to the leaves of plants; it was the kind of delicious linguistic tidbit that the Finn and I used to relish together.

The Finn's serious blue eyes look out of the photograph, taken not in New York but on the southwest coast of Finland near my family's summer cottage.

It was surprising how many near-clones of the Finn I found following her departure. On Broadway, a soaring woman with big hair turning at the curb to check for traffic: *her* face undulating at the end of the woman's long stalk. A crooked Ukrainian grandmother pushing a cart of parcels down the avenue: *she* in thirty years. The man behind the liquor store counter, ethnic background unknown, wisps of beard on his pointed chin: the chin like *hers*. The set of his lips as he focused, all her. Once in a while I even went so far as to reach out and touch the sleeve or shoulder of someone I believed was her, always to encounter the face of a stranger.

On the radio, a neurosurgeon being interviewed tells listeners that he has discovered, by placing electrodes on people's brains, that certain neurons light up when a person silently names an object to herself, but not, for instance, when reading the name of that object. The reverse is also true: some neurons only awaken when reading. In one bilingual patient, he found neurons that lit up when the patient was stimulated in Finnish but remained dormant when she was offered English.

I look at the Finn's photograph. What would I say if we were to ever meet again—*you manipulative little slime-mushroom; you crafty, passive-aggressive, thick-neck stevedore*, in English; or perhaps, after all, in Finnish, *the spouse of my golden days, my last and best bride?*

After all these years, my thoughts go to her as if to a summer fair: it's Sunday, the streets are empty, scraps of refuse spin lazily at the sewer's mouth, a beer bottle from the night before lies in shards on the asphalt. The sun is at its zenith. I step around the corner, toward her, and all of a sudden, harmonicas are playing— Anttila's Spring Fever song, *Anttilan keväthuumaus, juokse sinä humma kun tuo taivas on niin tumma*, and stalls are bursting with t-shirts and fairground trinkets and tin-foil-and-hay yo-yo balls in every color, and people are full of joy and hope and dressed in their spring finest.

I open my eyes, and I am in New York.

—

We met twenty-one years ago this fall, in 1995, after I had just moved in with Mare, my all-American girlfriend whom I'd met at college in Michigan. It was through Mare that I learned about America—to interpret its humor, analyze its politics, and understand its customs. It was Mare who explained the jokes on *SNL* until I got them on my own, Mare who taught me to make tuna casserole and cheeseballs, Mare who laughed at my earnest Finnish adherence to rules like not crossing the street on red.

Mare and I were still in the process of falling in love when I moved to New York, and I returned to Michigan as often as I could to complement our long-distance phone calls.

Falling in love with her, I fell in love with America.

Imagine a midwestern midnight. You have just made love.

In the aromatic night, you open the door of her pickup, start the engine, roll down the windows, and drive down a deserted highway. The smooth road hums beneath your wheels, and far away, beyond the fields, the lights of the city glow and all around you the meadows sigh in the fragrant dark.

That's what it was like, in Mare's America. In our America.

When Mare followed me to New York, she moved in with me to the apartment above the Indian restaurant, where in the mornings we woke to the smell of food preparation from the restaurant below. The smells reached our apartment all day long from both above and below; we were sandwiched between the restaurant and the apartment, where the kitchen staff bunked as well as fried the day's onions.

Mare and I were still new, and we made love incessantly; in the morning, before showering or after it, before lunch or after it, instead of dinner, upon going to bed. Sex eat sleep, sex eat sleep.

To celebrate the joining of our single lives, we threw a house-warming party in our apartment and invited everyone we knew.

We were receiving our guests in what we called our "third room," a tiny square of hallway that was all doors and almost no wall surface, the doors leading to the bedroom, living room, bathroom, kitchen, two closets, and out of the apartment itself. Between the bedroom and living room stood a narrow telephone stand—back then we still used an apparatus plugged into the wall, along with an answering machine, the technological advancement of the day.

The small apartment was full of the chatter of our two dozen guests, and we didn't hear the telephone. The volume on the answering machine had been turned up though, perhaps by the accidental brush of someone's sleeve. All of a sudden, right behind me, a voice I did not recognize sputtered out of the speaker. "Hello? Hello?" it said, over Ella Fitzgerald on the phonograph.

The accent was pared down, a sans serif of dialects, and the speaker's gender ambiguous. Everyone hushed and turned to stare at the machine, which issued a dense hum and garbled breathing. "I am outside," the voice said. A harsh click concluded the message.

Mare rushed downstairs and returned with a woman in her mid-to-late thirties in what used to be called a man's suit jacket but is now increasingly only called "a suit jacket." She was solidly built, her sparse hair thrusting forth like *rairuoho*, the Easter grass we grew in square vats all through Finnish grade school. As soon as I saw the face above the turned-up collar and the thin, fine hair, I recognized a fellow Finn.

Mare bounced on her heels and wrung her hands with excitement—she had landed on something special, introducing two fellow Finns to each other in a foreign country. She looked from me to the Finn and back, witness to this reunion of compatriots, as the woman and I made our way through halting introductions.

I had immersed myself into America so fully, succumbing to its soft, rolling English with such abandon, that encountering someone from my country of origin felt like a kind of violation.

I hadn't been to Finland in eight years, almost never spoke the language in New York, and considered myself fully integrated. I had long since stopped checking American tree trunks for authenticity, scratching with my nail to see whether it left a mark, as I had done during my first year. I had seen the leaves of the trees grow and fall and grow again, had missed their green shadows in the desolation of winter. I was *here*. This was real. Finland was a souvenir.

I had no interest in immigrant nostalgia or fresh news from the home front, so when Mare left the two of us to talk—"You must have so much to share," she said as she went—the timbre of the evening changed and a heaviness settled over me.

The Finn stood silent, as all around us others resumed their conversations and Ella moved on to "Mack the Knife."

In eschewing small talk, Finland as a nation seems unparalleled, but my Americanization demanded I at least attempt to draw out this guest, whose eyes seemed the only live part of her— they darted around and studiously avoided mine.

On my initiative, we disposed of talk of the weather (unseasonably hot), the date of and reason for her arrival in New York (two weeks ago; visiting scholar) and the expected duration of her stay (eight months).

What about you, she asked. "Entä sä?"

The language felt terse and blunt in comparison with the warm bath of English. "What about me?" I asked.

"How often do you go back?" Her eyes finally found mine.

"I don't." I used the consonant 'k' like a weapon: *En mä käy*.

She asked where I was from, as if that might explain my lack of travel. Out of a habit that predated my immigration, I hesitated. "The southwest. Near Turku."

In Finland, the Turku region, for both its coarse dialect and inward identity, is the New Jersey of America, or the Cork of Ireland. It is an affiliation one utters with both pride and chagrin.

There is no other word for the Finn's reaction—she cackled.

Here we go, I thought. Whenever I mentioned the town of my birth to an American, the response was pleasingly ignorant. Whenever I mentioned it to a fellow Finn, depending on the expat's own status in the hierarchy of Finnish geography, the response alternated between delight if the person hailed from the same region, or amused tolerance, if they did not, as in *You're from Turku and you* admit *it?*

"Originally, my family is Karelian," I hastened to amend.

"Mine too," she said. "Grandmother. Paternal."

Karelian ancestry was a genuine matter of pride. Karelians had been ejected from southeast Finland by the Soviets and resettled all over Finland during and after the Second World War. Few things could make a Finn tear up, but Lost Karelia was one.

"Grandmother, grandfather, both maternal," I replied. "Mikä maa, isänmaa, mikä isä, taivaanisä..." Which land, fatherland, which father, heavenly father. It was the beginning of a ditty I had learned from my grandmother, who'd had a lyric or saying for every occasion.

"...mikä taivas, enkelitaivas," the Finn said—which heaven, angel heaven.

This was an improvement over the conversations I had endured with other expatriate Finns with whom I'd attempted to socialize. Their first questions, invariably, addressed marital status. *Ootsä naimisis*—are you married—or, *Onks sul mies*—do you have a man. And: *Onks sul lapsii*—any children?

As we talked, it transpired we had both spent childhood summers on the same southwestern coast, mere miles apart. Even in Finland I'd never met anyone who had seen those secluded shores, and here I was, in Manhattan, speaking to someone who knew the name of the woman who operated the summer grocery near my family's cottage; who had, as I had, trespassed to climb to the top of the abandoned lighthouse on Työkinkari; and who could name the two unmarked dirt roads that forked at the base of the village.

A vein opened and I saw her already sailing toward me.

Mare, returning to check up on her experiment, saw it too, and for a moment, her face registered something besides excitement. She self-corrected, but doubt remained in her eyes from that moment on, whenever she and I saw the Finn.

For the first time since arriving in America I felt my two worlds, the past and the present, coming together. As the Finn and I conversed in Finnish, Mare came up behind me every now and then, placing her hands on my hips and standing silently while she listened to the language she couldn't understand. My body responded to the warmth of her hands, but my mind was beguiled by the mosaic of memories conjured by the Finn: of the northern sky over the archipelago, of a fox in winter, of lingonberries in September, of thieving seagulls snatching custards out of children's hands, of Karelian grandmothers dyeing Easter eggs with onion peels. Every one of these things I had forgotten.

—

A week after the party, Mare and I were having dinner at the Indian restaurant below our apartment.

"Chicken Vindaloo," we said in unison to the waiter.

"Oh no, it is too spicy," he said.

"We like spicy."

The waiter and the sweaty chef snickered behind the counter as we ate. The dish really was too hot, but we couldn't give up in front of the two men and emptied our plates with the help of water and mango lassi. Mare looked at me with tears in her eyes and stuck her tongue out to air it, and I thought she was almost unbearably seductive.

Afterwards, on the red door of our pre-war building, we discovered a handwritten note, unsigned and addressed to no one.

CAME BY 19.47. TRY AGAIN LATER

I knew right away who had left it. Only a Finn's ingrained discretion would reach such heights as to not only omit the names of the note's recipients (for reasons of privacy and/or uncertainty regarding correct spelling) as well as the note writer's own name (out of a shyness solidified into determined awkwardness), but also to insist, in the face of overwhelming American practice, on expressing the time of day in what in Finland was known as the European format. The Finn had recorded her precise moment of arrival.

Mare took the note. "Is that military time?"

"No, real time." I meant it as a wry sort of joke—*too real* was what I meant. Since the party, I had felt a new low-grade stress that I linked to the Finn. Seeing the note made me realize I did not want to see her again.

Mare pulled me upstairs. We exchanged curry kisses in the third room, and later, when her vindaloo tongue flickered down me, I moaned out loud—it was as if she were wielding an ember.

The doorbell rang.

Mare raised her head. I pushed it back as the heat spread through my tissues. I thrashed in spectacular pain and came faster than ever. We switched positions on the fly, and I thought: *Jaettu ilo, kaksinkertainen ilo*, a Finnish saying that meant "shared joy, double joy," and fell into Mare's silky surfaces as she gripped the sheet with both hands and the doorbell rang over and over.

Over the course of the night, after the buzzer had fallen silent, the stomach cramps began, and in the morning after a cup of coffee, my entire digestive system was dragged over live coals as the last burning kiss of vindaloo left my body.

—

The next evening, the doorbell rang again, and this time Mare answered.

I was in the shower when I heard the Finn's voice and, darting through the hallway into the bedroom in a towel, I saw Mare and the Finn sitting across from each other at the kitchen table.

After I had dressed I joined them, leaning against the gas range on the slanting, chessboard-patterned linoleum while the two of them chatted about university life. I did not interrupt but occupied myself with preparing the next day's work lunch—boiling an egg and washing salad ingredients as though we did not have a visitor. The whole time I was aware of being observed, taken in, by the Finn. I felt a growing aversion—the Finn was so *Finnish*—shy yet jaunty, sitting there *like that*—as if she had a special right to be there, to show up uninvited and sit down at our table. A bit rude, a bit of a redneck…The formula of my love life: two thimblefuls of distaste, one brimming with attraction.

Mare rose and suggested drinks at the corner bar. In my confusion, I forgot to remove the egg from the gas. Half an hour later, returning for cigarettes, I smelled the fumes from the door. In the smoky kitchen, the blackened kettle was doing a jig on the stove, a pea-sized coal hopping on the reacted aluminum.

The apartment stank for days after her visit.

—

The Finn affixed many notes on our red door that fall and winter, swiping curled-up scraps of tape from fliers posted on the payphone, always noting her arrival to the minute and in four digits.

We took her on as a friend but fought about her from the start. Though at first it was I who did not want her with us—because of the invasion of another Finn in my self-made universe—later it was Mare, because of the threat she perceived. The Finn rang the buzzer, we offered her a bed to sleep in and coffee in the morning. When I opened the door for her, she often said nothing and merely glanced at me as she walked in and deposited her backpack in the hallway. Without waiting for encouragement, she strode into the bedroom, the living room, or the kitchen, where she always sat down in Mare's chair, even after she had been to our apartment half a dozen times and knew for certain whose chair she was lowering her rear onto.

She reminded me of my grandmother, behaving as though she were an unwilling side character even at her own birthday party while never ceasing to maneuver from the sidelines, always in full control.

At parties and gatherings, the Finn was shy and stood in a doorway, her gaze seeking the farthest back corner of the room, where she would slip to the side—behind the table with the bar, on a windowsill—out of sight, out of the way of the action. She believed that everyone else, especially every American, was louder, stronger, bolder, more extroverted, aggressive and space-occupying than she. But when the party was over and others had left, she remained, because she was so small and insignificant that she couldn't possibly be a disturbance.

And always we let her stay.

—

Despite the spicy bliss of our East Village honeymoon, I began to see the relationship between Mare and me from a dual perspective: in English and in American terms, and in Finnish and in Finnish terms. I wasn't only *in* the relationship anymore—I now also saw it as if from the outside, from a vantage point not *of here*.

At the corner bar, during a live performance of a Norwegian rune singer, Mare fidgeted next to me. She looked at people out of the corner of her eye and grimaced. "This music," she whispered, her hot breath in my ear, her body twitching as if she had an itch that had to be attended. I held my finger to my lips.

Mare had been born in the West and was used to open vistas and sun and bluegrass. She would have rather two-stepped, knees in the air, elbows out, than listen to this music that seemed only to make people serious and sad.

"What should we have for dinner, darling?" she asked during a break between the sets.

"Indian?"

"No…Don't feel like it, my love." She had endless pet names for me.

"How about Vietnamese?"

Her pretty features distorted. "Not that either, dear-heart."

—

The Finn and I spent more and more time together, meeting in the city on Thursday nights while Mare taught at the university, or meeting at her cottage, a commuter train ride away from the City.

Her tiny house was perched under an ancient elm and surrounded by soft grass, and compared to the East Village, the place was pastoral. From the first visit, occupying the silence of the semi-rural neighborhood brought us closer to Finland, and as she sat on the front step chewing a blade of foxtail—a scene repeated in countless Finnish films—America seemed to fall away. Her stillness, her slowness, sank into me.

For a long time, we simply watched a beetle wage combat with a plantain leaf.

"Rautalehti," she said of the greater plantain, and suddenly I recognized the plant, familiar from Finland, for the first time. Unknowingly, I had trampled on it in New York City parks without realizing it was the same one I had grown up with. Afterwards I looked up the English word in a dictionary.

For most New Yorkers, "greater plantain" might not be a vessel for transmitting ancient knowledge; it awakens no memory of a grandmother's rough hands touching your baby skin, her strong fingers winding a blade of grass around the pliant plantain leaf wrapped around your small fingers, to shield the neat cuts slashed into your soft flesh after you picked up the scythe by its blade, honed lethal against her lump of whetstone and just lying on the ground—because you wanted to help.

Koivikko, kataja, metsälampi, lumme. Would you be my birch cove, my juniper, my forest pond or woodland lily?

I began to think of the Finn more and more, even when Mare and I made love. *She* would stare relentlessly from the bookcase between G. Stein and V. Woolf, cut off at the neck like a cheap Halloween trick, while Mare held my absent body. I wasn't sure whose rhythm I was moving to, and as Mare stroked my spine and pressed against me, her hot lips at my ear, *she* asked challengingly from the bookcase, how does it feel? *Miltä nyt tuntuu?*

I breathed over Mare's shoulder in the dark, forcing myself not to stop in the middle of the lovemaking, cheering myself on. A salmon must feel the same as it swims upstream.

Mare got up to use the bathroom. Waiting for her, I turned my behind toward the radiator to warm it up, for her, for Mare, trying to banish the Finn.

Mikä enkeli, musta enkeli.

Which angel, black angel.

—

By November, I was riding the train to the cottage nearly every week.

The Finn was not surprised when I mentioned you could cure rickets with the leaves of the red elderberry, the "shit tree." This is not information one needs here, now, but my grandmother had applied the leaves to my mother's parenthetic legs to straighten them during the lean war years, and the Finn was the only person in my world who knew the significance of every element of that statement. She nodded when I said, in passing, that seeing a mourning cloak butterfly in the morning meant someone would die that day—on my grandfather's day of leaving, my grandmother had encountered the black-and-white wings on her walk to the well.

The melding of the Finn and my grandmother's memories in the present gave rise to cognitive distortions that began to plague me in the midst of everyday living.

A woman waiting for a train on a subway platform. *One more step*, whispered a voice.

A burn mark on a cheek—someone has put out their cigarette on it.

A scythe slices off a nipple.

A darning needle extinguishes the convex gleam of an eye.

The terror of heights, the suck of the deep.

Who used a scythe when I was small? My grandmother. A darning needle? Same woman. Who walked me to the edge of a precipice, where the emptiness below breathed with the force of a vacuum of space?

What looked beautiful on the outside—our Finnish friendship—was as rotten on the inside as the putrid pulp inside my grandmother's hand-dyed Easter egg, when the shell finally broke. I knew the Finn wanted more than friendship.

—

Mare and I were sitting on the concrete steps in Union Square, facing the last warmth of the December sun and the bumper-to-bumper traffic on 14th Street, waiting for the Finn. Two heads of cabbage lolled at my feet in a plastic bag; I was planning a stew—probably *her* presence in New York had inspired the idea. In our mutual childhoods, cabbage stew cooked in enormous cauldrons by burly cafeteria ladies and skinny, pimple-faced apprentices had been a cornerstone of Cold War school lunches.

When the Finn arrived, I was leaning against Mare with my eyes closed. Even before opening them, I felt someone else's body heat nearing. Mare was up first and held out her hand to pull me up, and in the moment it took for me to stand up the Finn managed to flash me a very quick, very lively look—like the reflection of the sun bouncing off a passing car: a momentary blinding.

Mikä musta, pikimusta
Mikä piki, suutarin piki
Which black, pitch black
Which pitch, cobbler's pitch

That evening, over drinks in our kitchen, it was settled that she would rent our second room for a week over Christmas while Mare went to visit her family in California.

Mare rose to fill our drinks from a bottle of cheap champagne, and when she opened the fridge, one of the cabbages rolled out of the I ♥ NY bag and lumbered down the slanting floor until it came to a rest in front of the Finn.

—

Aika rohkeeta—pretty gutsy, the Finn said to me, an angry, auburn Christmas moon behind her in the window.

What?

Risking a friendship like that by being together.

She was referring to the friendship between Mare and I before we fell in love.

By introducing the idea of the courageousness of our love, it was as though she had simultaneously introduced the possibility of its failure. If it was gutsy, it was risky.

I couldn't do it, she said.

Fall in love with a friend?

Fall in love in English, she said.

Why not?

It wouldn't be true.

A kiss is true.

A kiss and suudelma are not the same thing.

A kiss is a kiss. It's bodies talking to each other, I replied.

Your body doesn't have a language?

—

On New Year's Eve, the day of Mare's return from California, the Finn was gone. I lay on the futon staring at the parquet floor the way one stares at a nearby detail, like the fold of a bed sheet—because it is there and because it doesn't require thought.

My feet wouldn't stop whisking.

When Mare came home and we kissed hello, something had changed. The kiss was objectively a good kiss, but its fullness had dwindled, become half.

Mikä suutari, kenkäsuutari, mikä kenkä, puolikenkä.

Which cobbler, shoe cobbler, which shoe, half shoe.

—

"I feel more towards you than just friendship," the Finn mumbled one night in late January, pressing her cheek against the brass bar top. It was Thursday night, *our* night.

The grin crept across my face like algae. I tried to stop it, but it only spread. We lingered in the bar for a long time, and when I finally went home, an angry Mare met me at the door. I felt the grin stretching my face, it wouldn't succumb to orders from the frontal lobe.

I walked into her arms, we kissed. I smiled and told her that the Finn was in love with me. I couldn't stop the algae.

"Is she. What are you telling me that for?"

"I wanted to tell you, I couldn't not. It's why I'm late."

"So when will you two start going out?"

"I don't want to be with her, silly. I told her I didn't feel the same."

"When's your next date?"

On Thursday. From then on, mostly in secret. But even after I had come home in the early morning hours, smelling of hops and dragging the breaking news onto our doormat, entrails and all, the Finn still came a few times. For her last visit she bought black salmiakki, salt licorice, from the Dutch candy store down the street, and offered it to me but not to Mare. Like an idiot I sucked on the salty round, feeling special because she wasn't as rude to me as to Mare.

She didn't stay the night. Mare had lost all motivation to be hospitable—the salmiakki had been offered (only to me) and she had been shown her place too many times (the Finn knew it was Mare's chair).

—

"You're not going to see that water lily again," Mare said the morning after the licorice, as I was handing her the top half of a toasted everything bagel.

I sat down.

"And can you please take care of those crumbs," she said and nodded at the seeds and bagel remnants on the cutting board. "Seriously, clean up first, otherwise we won't enjoy eating."

In the name of détente, I dumped the crumbs in the trash. We ate in silence until I got up and went to the fridge to pour myself a glass of water from the filter canister. I replaced the pitcher and sat down.

Mare put her bagel on her plate. "You're not going to refill the water canister?"

"I'll do it later—it's almost full."

"You really should fill the canister every time you use it."

"It's my fucking canister." It was true—I had gone to great trouble in building all the trappings of a normal life, of a home; I'd had to, in order to feel grounded in America. Physical details like rugs and water pitchers meant nothing to Mare, whose things were in storage in California, near her family. She had brought nothing but her books to our household.

—

People's stories have a tendency to repeat themselves, get stuck in a loop. Loss is a skill we learn only gradually. As we begin to understand love better and more profoundly, we learn to be let down with ever greater finesse.

Five years old, standing in the dark hallway of our apartment building, I reach for the yellow light button on the wall. Should I go to the playground via the cellar, that way is shorter, without having to leave the building and walk all the way around it. But I'm afraid of the dark and decide to take the long way, via the sidewalk, via the light.

Outside I glimpse my best friend Tuomas disappearing around the corner. I run toward the sun, toward him, and catch up, a smile already tugging at the corners of my mouth, when I stop short. A girl from the building next door is with him. Together they measure me and yell in unison even as they run backwards toward the playground and the swings. *Lillillillilieru, sulta pääsi pieru!* Na-na-na-na-na-naa! You let out a faaart!

I retrace my steps and go home, dragging my body against the cool stone wall as I climb the stairs back up, stopping on the windowed landings to gaze down to where Tuomas and the girl swing lazily.

Life lesson Number One: you can lose anything with no warning.

Inside, my grandmother asks, wasn't there anyone else there? I shake my head no and draw a picture of our family. It's one of my best: father, mother, children, cat. Here we are, a whole real family.

I hear Tuomas's mother calling him inside and check through the window for the girl. She's gone. It's my turn to swing.

When I come back in at dusk my parents are home, and I'm dying to show off the drawing, but no one can find it. Finally my father asks what I am looking for and I tell him and his face sags.

"Damn it to hell, how could I have known it was such an important drawing!" He sighs as he watches the grey cat in its feeding nook. It's licking its paws after a meal of herring, one of them planted in the middle of the drawing, covered in fish scales.

Life lesson Number Two: each subsequent loss is merely a mimeograph shadow of the first disappointment. Once the domino effect has begun, nothing will ever stop it.

—

I had not intended to be drunk when the Finn came.

Waiting at an empty Middle Eastern restaurant, chosen for the view it afforded of the street corner where we were to meet, I chatted with the waiter. He gave me a glass of white wine on the house after I found a large moth in the mesclun. He also offered to replace the salad. But moths were part of the tapestry in Finland, bumping silently in the corners of window frames, clamped in floury triangles in the folds of curtains. I insisted on keeping my salad despite the waiter's raised eyebrows.

He lingered, telling me he was in the middle of a divorce, though he had been happily married until his wife's mother had died the previous year. She had asked for a divorce immediately after the funeral. "It just doesn't add up," he said.

I sipped on the white wine and disagreed but saw no point in telling him that. His wife's internal reality had shifted, and she had understood that the reality she had been living had not really "penetrated"—it didn't match what was inside her. But her mother was real, and now also dead, and it was time for the wife to find the truth that matched her internal landscape. I thought about Mare, teaching in midtown, unaware that I was meeting the Finn.

Out of the corner of my eye, I saw the Finn arrive at the corner and check the time on her wristwatch. She was early, and I finished my third glass of wine and settled up with the despondent waiter.

Outside, she stood facing the intersection. I tapped her on the shoulder and she turned, and I don't know how it happened or who did what, but her face was very close to mine and without saying anything she kissed me.

She kissed me multiple times, tiny little pecks, like fractions of a kiss, too tender to feed the tension that the daydreams of this moment had fed in me. I tried to catch the tail of one of those dreams, something about the *wind pivoting the leaves, grass glistening, she's taking off my shirt...*But it was no use, the connection between us stuttered.

An acquaintance had once offered me her view of sex between two women. She postulated that there would be a lot of tenderness and endless, rather asexual though erotic, touching, and most definitely copious amounts of caressing of the other's hair. Disinfected sex, clean as a Q-tip, not-quite-sex.

I thought about the robust kisses Mare and I shared, and I kissed the Finn back hard, to abolish the frustrating gentleness. She made a tiny squeak of pleasure, but I felt formless, bodyless.

We went into a bar. A couple sat near us, arguing, their faces strained as if trying to breathe in a garage filling with carbon monoxide. As we took our time to begin, first the woman left, and a moment later, soon enough so that he could still catch up with her if he wanted to, departed the angry-looking man.

"Love," the Finn said in Finnish and chuckled. *Rakkaus.*

"I've never liked that word," I said. "Like a cat coughing up a hairball."

She knotted her fingers into tight fists on the table. Comfortable hands, the hands of a small farmer. "Siulla on se ilme."

You have that look. The lilting Karelian of her *siulla*, "you," raised the hairs on my arms. "What look?"

"The one that says 'I've closed the gates.'"

"I can't see you anymore."

She rolled her eyes.

"I can't be both." I clarified: "Finnish and American. I have to be just one."

"So not Finnish then."

"I live here. My life is here."

"My life could be here."

No, I thought. It was mine, this life I had made. The Finnish awareness she had brought had only sown disorder.

Our eyes locked in the haze of the dive bar. This gaze would not be repeated with anyone else. *What do you see in her*, Mare had asked. This, the gaze.

Outside, we both stared at the same spot on the ground—a heap of broken glass, a scrap of paper towel, a crumpled pack of Marlboros. Two Finns in a Manhattan night. She turned and walked away.

I watched her retreating back. *Mikä puoli, takapuoli.* Which half, ass half.

Mare was asleep when I crawled into bed next to her. I sounded out my body, that traitor, but it had nothing more to say.

—

One morning, in a cab on the expressway as we headed to the airport, I pointed out to Mare all the plastic bags I saw through the car window, floating in the wind.

"Bag."

"Another."

Next to me, Mare, whom I was accompanying to a conference, hmphhed and ignored me. As we began the turn onto the Brooklyn Bridge, a bird flew past us. It was a pigeon, white, body taut, stretched forward, pitching through the air like a fish, the speed making lace of its wings.

With me and the Finn and the pigeon it would have gone like this: one of us would have noticed the bird, the other's gaze would have followed that of the first, the bird would have flown past, we would have looked at each other and the bird would have commenced to exist in a new way, a tiny story between the two of us, a microscopic awareness, and together we would have wished the pigeon well, and I would have seen it through her eyes, she through mine, and a fleck of us would have flown with the bird to the other side of town, or the opposite side of the river, where maybe it had a rendezvous with another pigeon in a particular tree in front of a particular window of a particular apartment building, where it and the others waited for the old woman to appear between the curtains and fling seeds into the air out of her hand, and when the driver of a passing car glanced out of his or her window, the flock of pigeons burst in the air, their wings frothing into one another as they plunged after the seeds, beaks gaping, until they had vacuumed the seeds from the air and returned to their stations on the limbs of the tree, and the driver of the passing car would already be veering onto the bridge and smiling without knowing why, as he or she left Manhattan and the bridge rose, mammoth and melodramatic as a movie backdrop. When the bird flew past us.

—

It was Tax Day, in April, when Mare left, right after she found a ticket to a concert I had gone to with the Finn on one of those Thursdays while she was working. Mare moved back to California, but first, for fourteen days and nights, we wrangled over it, morning till night. Why, how, with whom, but. She no longer trusted me, she said. Why, I wanted to know.

Because of *her* of course.

But I don't *love* her.

English words had been like empty storage boxes on a warehouse shelf, labeled and soulless, until I experienced what they held inside. Love, longing, despair, heartbreak.

During the day I went to work in Brooklyn and took long bathroom breaks on the 20th floor of my office building and watched the pigeons lined up along a ledge. They looked back at me as I confirmed for myself that if I leapt in a slight arc I would not in fact fall on top of the adjacent building but would go all the way down into the garbage dumpsters. Blup blup, said the pigeons, nodding. On the gym treadmill, sorrow battled endorphins, the tears winning at mile two. At home I raged and roared, throwing boots, magazines, anything, all over the room, without hitting anything, without breaking anything. Mare ran to me and held me the way a mover holds a heavy bureau in a stairwell: if this falls, it will crush me too.

Night after night, after she left, I drank wine in front of the television, set to a channel with only static, and daydreamed of a cottage in the countryside, of trees and grass and a winding road, maybe a vegetable garden, a sunny patch of gravel, a small child with the setting sun in her hair.

I opened my eyes, and I was in New York. Upstairs the Indian men clattered dishes and fried onions and once in a while broke into raucous laughter. I was alone with my Finnish.

P.S. KATE

EVER SINCE THE TIP OF HER LEFT BREAST WAS SLICED OFF WHEN she was seventeen, in a freak accident during a family visit to Latvia and Finland, Kate had known that life was uncontrollable. She only remembered the moment before, standing in her grandmother's shady garden in Latvia, and the moment after, when she saw her mother's face and fainted. Then, the municipal health center, and hearing her mother and the stranger that was her grandmother speaking the language that her mother never used at home in New Jersey.

There was no nipple there, only a slightly puckered plane from the crude stitching done at the clinic, and sometimes, like now, as she balanced on the F train and tried not to touch the handlebars, a long-dormant nerve would send a sharp twinge to the apex of her breast to remind her of the old injury. She brushed her fingers over her breast, feeling the odd, airy void at the tip, after the breast button she taped there as a replacement had fallen into the office toilet when she was changing into a nicer top and bra, for Jason's party. It was the eve of her 39th birthday and he had planned a surprise.

She was always losing the ersatz nipple, starting with the decorative button she had taken from her grandmother's sewing basket on the trip to Latvia. That one she lost at a college drinking party, and she was constantly searching for a better, more perfect button or broken seashell swirl to fill the void. Before her mother died, she had tried to convince Kate to have plastic surgery to reshape the crown of her breast, but she was used to it. The injury was an external manifestation of the loss and precarity that were part of life anyway.

Sometimes she wondered if her grandmother had ever found the missing part of her in the garden—if she had, no one had told her. And how would you? "I found your nipple in the garden. Do you still want it?"

After large family of tourists got out at West 4th Street, Kate spotted an empty seat and made for it, then stopped short: someone had spilled coffee there. At every stop, another commuter saw the seat, strode toward it, then turned away as though never intending to sit there in the first place, until East Broadway, when a woman of about twenty lunged for the seat, noticed the coffee spatters at the very last moment and sat down anyway, half-perching on the molded plastic, with a pained expression. That was the kind of person the girl was, Kate thought: after starting the motion to sit down, she was too embarrassed to change course.

A man positioned himself directly in front of the girl. He grasped the bar above with both hands, his body—his groin—swinging inches from the girl's face. This was why Kate generally preferred to stand.

She put in her earbuds and undid the plastic clip that held up her shoulder-length hair at the office, but didn't shake her hair out immediately, so that as the train jolted underneath the East River and the Sibelius violin concerto swelled in her ears, the coil of her hair came undone in a slow caress that she gave herself for the commute home. The album was one her father had begun playing on the turntable after his mother's death; Kate had downloaded the music after her latest visit to his nursing home, eager for some connection to her family and her past. She enjoyed the privacy of having the concerto's familial associations traveling alongside her even as she was surrounded by strangers.

She considered the riders with whom she'd be making this journey every day for the foreseeable future; today, on the three-month anniversary of her temp assignment, she had been offered a permanent position. She was finally on her way to something solid.

Next to her, a woman with sad eyes and a broad, flat behind held onto the center pole as the train picked up speed. How different the behinds of cave women must have been, instead of the wide buttocks flattened by office chairs and subway seats. She debated whether the woman was pro- or anti-gun: her fabric tote was printed with weapons of various shapes, colors and sizes.

Guns were something she had never thought about much until Jason.

—

They had met six years earlier on the southwest corner of Fifth Avenue and 18th Street in Manhattan. She had been waiting for the light to change when a man said:

"Excuse me."

She was startled—since the nipple accident, she was highly sensitive to whatever approached her from the left side and easily startled by ordinary things, like a person walking toward her or a car turning, but she had not sensed this man coming.

He was trim and middle-aged and held a cane for the visually impaired and stood right at the curb, facing north.

"Do you need help?" She sought his eyes in spite of herself, though he was wearing dark glasses.

"Can you help me across the street?"

"Of course."

He stepped closer. "I'll take your arm, if you don't mind."

"No, not at all," she said but thought: a man is a man. He

could be a blind lech, or pretending to be visually impaired to prey on women.

"Where are you headed," she asked, his arm looped around hers.

"To the subway. Union Square. Can you take me there?"

She had to be at her doctor's office in the East Village in fifteen minutes. She picked up the pace. He didn't seem to mind. "Are you coming from the Library for the Visually Impaired?" she asked. It was on the same block as her office.

"No, from the shooting range."

She examined his face for signs of subterfuge. Was he joking? He didn't look like he was. "Interesting," she said, careful.

"It's called acoustic shooting—I picked it up a few years ago. It hones my ability to navigate based on sound."

She still wasn't sure he was telling the truth but decided to go with it. "It's amazing what the brain is capable of."

"Yes." They rounded the corner of Broadway and 18th Street, the sidewalk crowded with tourists and office workers. "Ballroom dancing's another thing I picked up, for the same reason. Do you dance?"

"Ballroom? No." She wondered if he would ask her out. What would she say? You could go, she thought, daring herself.

"So what do you do?" he asked instead.

"I'm a graphic designer." Actually she reproduced other people's layouts at marketing agencies.

"Ah." He seemed unimpressed. "Are we almost there?"

"Let's cross here." She stepped into the street, pausing to give him a chance to step off the curb with her. The Union Square greenmarket was open, and hundreds of people milled in front of the stalls and awnings. They reached the subway stairs and she waited until he had a hold of the railing.

"Thank you, I appreciate this," he said.

He hadn't asked her to go ballroom dancing. He hadn't even

asked her name. She felt her face redden. At least he couldn't see it.

One week later she returned to the corner of Fifth Avenue and 18th Street at lunchtime and waited for the man to reappear. He did. Like last time, he stopped at the edge of the curb and turned to face uptown. She closed her eyes and realized how he knew to stop: the roar of traffic down Fifth Avenue was obvious. She was moved and intrigued.

When she opened her eyes he was in front of her. The terrifying tang of new love settled over her.

She had always fallen in love sure-fire fast, and once the process had begun, there was nothing she could do to stop it. On their first date, hurrying toward each other at the agreed-upon meeting place by Union Square's Gandhi statue, he kicked her big toe and tore off the nail. She recoiled, trying to muffle her yelp of pain, and he took her struggle for a sign of passion. He smiled and grasped her hand and led her across the street to the expensive café where she had never been and in whose elegantly scented restroom she ran cold water over her blood-soaked sandal and toe, the nail hanging by a thread.

—

Before dusk, on 7th Avenue in Brooklyn, she walked to kill time until the party, passing the new sustainable toy store, the frozen yogurt place, the boarded-up travel agency. In front of the hair salon she stopped to watch two pigeons fucking on the ledge above the awning. Beat—beat—half-beat—finished. That's how it was with her and Jason now. He would grab her by the hair and push her into a wall and fuck her, and she let him. Inside the salon, Emma, her stylist, sat in a barber's chair. She looked up from her phone and gestured to Kate.

Why not go in? She had more than an hour to herself and had been meaning to make an appointment for a touch-up.

She could be fashionably late for the party.

"You want the usual? Cut and color?"

Kate looked at her reflection in the mirror, at the corners of her mouth and the beginnings of the jowls that her mother had had, and her mother before her. How was it that she had become so boring? That was how someone looking at her on the subway would see her, the same way she had observed the flat-assed woman with the sad eyes and the perching girl. She looked at Emma's punked-out pixie and fringe. "I think I want something different—new, more like—like Miley Cyrus?"

Emma raised her plucked eyebrows but set to mixing the color. While she applied the paste, Kate flipped through an old issue of *Vogue*. Her phone rang; it was Jason, checking on her timing. She told him another forty-five minutes, and then told him about the ad agency's offer.

"What did you say?" Jason's voice was accompanied by the usual crackling on the line. They had different phone carriers whose networks clashed, and neither had been willing to switch to the other's carrier.

"I said yes. I need the money." She remembered the managing director's boundlessly excited face as he described the salary and benefits, and how he clapped his hands at her response: "Oh yay! We love Shadow Kate!"

She wondered if her name was the reason she'd been selected from the temp agency's roster in the first place—there were three others at the office with basically the same name—another Kate, a Katie and a Kat, all of whom lived in Brooklyn, like she did. To differentiate her from them she was known as Park Slope Kate, for her section of the borough. This had gradually morphed to "P.S. Kate," and finally she herself began to sign off on internal documents with just *P.S.*, even though she suspected there was a sly joke, or an insult, contained in how the name had stuck, but couldn't identify exactly what—something about her being an afterthought.

"We have money, Kate," Jason was saying. "What we don't have is time. It's going to be way more stressful for you."

Stressful. She envisioned the office, coated with the dust of foregone successes, its clientele—she had been told this at the watercooler—down to two from about twenty. Several of the open-plan rooms had only a single Pandora-listening tumbleweed sitting behind his or her desk, waiting for retirement. Like the copyeditor who regularly came into her cubicle to complain that she wasn't using the correct format for document codes, the tiny series of letters and numbers in the corners of all the layouts that no one ever looked at except for the copyeditor, reading the codes out loud to himself in his windowless room.

"Your migraines might come back," Jason was saying. "Plus, you won't have time for your *work*."

She actually had a headache now. As for her "work," Jason was referring to the screenplay she had been writing with her film-school friend Terrance for at least five years. "Listen, I'm not in a good place…"

"And we'll never be able to go on vacation—" Jason's voice was cut off by the door buzzer. It was the wine delivery for the party—she had picked up the phone the night before when the store called to confirm their address. She heard the digital cacophony of Jason's cellphone knocking against things as he accepted the delivery. They had never gone on vacation in their four years together, and now that his public radio talk show was taking off, they wouldn't get away for more than a weekend anyway.

"Time to rinse," Emma said.

"Jason?" She hung up.

While Emma applied the toner, her phone kept ringing across the room. She was taken aback by Jason's resistance. Jason, who was visually impaired after a degenerative disease had left him almost totally blind by age eleven, and who was much more ambitious and confident than she was, nevertheless had a neediness that perplexed her. At home he would stand in front of the refrigerator and demand: "What's this?" so that she would have to walk over to see what he was pointing at. He was always asking to be buzzed in instead of using his key, or to have her meet him at the subway stop and walk home with him—he thought nothing of making her get dressed and leave the television show she was watching to go back into the wintry night to accompany him for the four blocks to their house. He said it was his way of showing his love.

Back in the chair, she saw three missed calls.

"Tilt your head, Kate." Emma started clipping.

Kate. Maybe she should take on a new name. Or her real one. It was actually Katarina, a nod by her Latvian mother and Finnish father to their respective countries of origin, but at home they had called her Kate and spoken English. She had been to Finland and Latvia only that one time, meeting both grandmothers, both widowed, both living in similar, red-painted cottages in the countryside. Neither of them had spoken English and both died when she was in college. Then, her mother died of an aneurysm in the beginning of her senior year, and now, her father had dementia and no longer recognized her. He had forgotten all about English and only spoke Finnish, baffling the staff at his Montclair nursing home.

"We've given you everything—you could be anything"—the words her parents had repeated all through her adolescence. They had ladled money and knowledge and information into her and nixed all of her own inclinations, to go to concerts with friends, study abroad, take theater lessons. After her mother's death she had gone into the army surplus store and bought a pair of black combat boots and, without telling her father, enrolled in all-film classes for her last two semesters, and switched her major.

But she hadn't made much of herself. Untethered to the parental leash, she had flailed.

That was the other reason she had been drawn to Jason: he held her so tightly inside his orbit that she always knew when she was straying out of bounds.

He was the only one who would care whether she had a job. She flipped through the magazine, full of office ensembles and cocktail dresses. She hated the thought of the birthday party: having to make her entrance, shriek "in surprise," pretend that dazed incomprehension that everyone expected. At least Terrance would be there, Terrance who, as she had slowly relinquished her cinematography dreams, had gone on to direct award-winning documentaries that she occasionally assisted on in a non-camera capacity, like a parasite nibbling at the creative froth of its host. And on this latest shoot, they'd suddenly had a moment, the kind they used to have as students at the end of a production, when it was all about to be over and the pent-up tension and effort all crested. But it had been only a moment, a quick look that could have gone somewhere but never did. Tonight, he would greet her the way he always did, kissing her on the lips so briefly that she barely registered it. She wondered if his wife Gianna noticed and if so, if it bothered her.

Kate felt the razor slide behind her left ear and up the side of her head. "Wait, what are you doing!"

In the mirror, Emma's eyes went wide and she stepped back from Kate as though from a burning object. "You said 'Miley Cyrus'..."

Kate stared at the shorn plow on the side of her head—like an airstrip for a small plane. "Not *that* Miley Cyrus, Miley Cyrus *now*!"

—

Several people on 7th Avenue smiled as they passed her—the kinds of people who hardly noticed her usually. It was as if she had been suddenly admitted to a secret club of artists and eccentrics, whereas the Brooks Brothers set looked right past her.

Outside the apartment door she had the fleeting thought that she should have brought something besides herself to the party. Jason had taught her not to show up "with her arms swinging" at someone's house; her reclusive parents had never instructed her about things like that.

Behind the door, she prepared her face for astonishment. And, in fact, she didn't know what to expect, or how many people. She opened the door slowly.

The first person she saw was Terrance, in the kitchen, his surprise mirroring her own. Since film school he hadn't seen her in anything but the bob whose length merely ebbed and flowed. But before they had a chance to greet each other, Jason bounded out of the living room. "There she is, me very own lass. Are you gobsmacked or what?"

He had embraced his fourth-generation Irish heritage and borrowed verbiage and accents freely from Irish, Welsh and British English, without discriminating. He hadn't thought or bothered to take the surprise all the way—turning off the lights and silencing the room before Kate entered. She waved at the dozen people— Jason's radio station friends, plus two couples they sometimes talked to at the neighborhood bar, and Terrance and Gianna.

Gianna grabbed Jason's elbow. "We had so much fun planning this! Happy birthday!"

Kate succumbed to her kiss and winked at Terrance, who gave her a glass of champagne. "Happy birthday, Rina," he said, using her college nickname. Gianna and Jason, faces flushed from the champagne, were delighted with themselves in the way of people who had managed to deceive a dear friend with the best of intentions.

Kate took a generous gulp as Gianna, Terrance and the others shuffled out onto the fire escape and up to the roof, to watch the last of the sunset.

Jason leaned in to kiss her. "Happy birthday, Katy-Kay." He put his hand on the back of her neck. "What the hell…"

"I got a haircut."

"It's—it feels like a man."

"Thanks." She shrank from his fingers.

"Wait, let me feel it."

As he traced her neck and the outlines of her face, she watched his dismay give way to excitement. She knew that expression; she used to love seeing Jason lose himself when they had sex, become entirely unguarded. At first there had been a kind of relief in his not seeing her—dancing, making love, eating, she could feel herself in a way that was different from anything she had ever experienced. She was freer to be present, her face unburdened by observation, merely part of the totality of skin, bones, cells and blood vessels, not the billboard promoting her her-ness to the world. She could retain a dimension of privacy, she'd thought, and avoid being seen—he would never look at her deadhead-nipple, criticize how she dressed, or see the dark circles around her eyes.

But by now she understood that he was as capable as anyone of seeing her—better, really. He noticed more, not less. His fingers saw her nipple, his ears told him her exact whereabouts in the apartment, and he heard and felt and smelled her mood, or what she was doing at any given time. When she used the bathroom, she turned on the faucet full force to block his echo-locating ears from picking up her noises.

Jason took off his sunglasses, which had left shiny half-moon dents below his eyes. Kate could see his pores so clearly. Was a relationship all over when one began to notice such things?

"Come." He took her by the hand.

"No, we can't…plus I'm exhausted," she said but allowed herself to be pulled along to the bedroom.

"It's OK, you don't have to do anything, babe." He sounded

resigned. "Hey, what happened—"

He had slipped his hand up her blouse.

"Don't ask," she said as his hand moved down from her breast and he pulled down her jeans (dark wash, in accordance with the agency's dress code). She held on to his biceps under the wool cardigan and closed her eyes, trying to recover a trace of the breathless need she used to feel as he pushed inside her. A phrase that someone had uttered at that morning's New Business Meeting came to her: high-impact push-down sponsorship. She laughed out loud, her abdominal muscles contracting against Jason's urgent grinding.

—

Up on the roof, Kate flipped her new fringe of hair and watched the last of the setting sun burnishing the old water towers and industrial structures of the Gowanus. She didn't know Jason's work friends very well, so she chatted with Gianna and the neighborhood friends. The champagne had gone to her head, she'd had four glasses, and she kept blurting things out in the middle of the convivial chitchat. Normally shy, she turned feisty when drunk.

At some point she left the group to go downstairs to the bathroom, careful on the fire escape but buoyant. In these heady, alcohol-fueled moments she often felt on the verge of something, with a sense of balancing on a fence, about to tip over either back into the familiar or, perilously, into the unknown, the side where she knew she was meant to be but that seemed as far from the realm of the possible as the coast of Siberia.

In the bright light of the bathroom, she smiled at her reflection, her cheeks blooming, her eyes shining. The stylist had convinced her it was better to shave the left side of her head entirely and keep the right side longer. The end result wasn't bad—it was crazy. She'd never had hair like this. She really did feel on the verge—what else could she do that she hadn't before? Get an actual film job? Ride a Greyhound across the country? Get a tattoo? Travel, to Finland and Latvia…

She was still smiling when she opened the door and felt that alert sensation on her left side.

Terrance was standing in the hallway, in the dark. "I was looking for you. I have to go, I have a work thing." He leaned toward her the way he always did, to kiss her goodbye, and she let his lips reach hers and he began to pull back, or maybe he didn't—he didn't—he stayed where he was, and it was her job to pull back, but this time, after all the hundreds of times they had greeted each other or said goodbye like this, she didn't pull back—and her lips did what lips do, but only for a second, and they pulled apart—she pushed him away in fact, and they stood in the hallway, the distant voices of their friends floating down from the roof.

Terrance's phone rang and he turned away to speak while she closed her eyes and felt the blood flooding her hips and pelvis.

"Oh Rina." He had hung up.

In the dim glow of the bathroom nightlight she saw how absolutely beautiful he was. But no, no, it was never going to happen, and now they had to begin the gargantuan task of repairing what had been done.

Terrance had a look of almost cinematic chagrin. "I'm sorry."

"Shut up." It was all running away from her.

"It's not—"

"That kiss," she shook her head, "it was just birthday cake."

He looked at her, knowing, recognizing, disbelieving, cranky. "I don't know."

The whole time she was dying to take just that one further step, make one more gesture, give him one brief glimpse of a molten look. But he was her friend and this was not their life. They hugged and she extricated herself, trying to walk back from the swell of desire.

It was all wrong, yet it felt incredible. She hadn't felt anything like this in so long. In the bright light of the kitchen, she downed a glass of Sauvignon Blanc and, swaying with wine, headed to the fire escape and pitched forward too fast and lifted her head too early and smashed it spectacularly against the window frame. The pain was sickening, her eyes filled with water and everything spun. She crawled onto the rusted structure on her hands and knees and huddled in the dark, blinking slowly, open, shut, like the sleep eyes of a doll being turned over, and waited for the pain to subside.

Afterwards, she couldn't remember anything else of that evening.

—

She was happy was all she knew when she awoke.

A dust particle, long as a polyp, twisted and turned in the air in front of her, in a thick cone of white morning sunlight. It was part of a swarm of specks, like dandelion fluff, or mosquitoes on a summer night. *Focus long enough and I will open my doors to you*, the speck whispered and twinkled enticingly. A door opened and she had the impression that something momentous had happened, but she couldn't identify what or when. Had she received important news? Had an encounter with someone? An altercation, a fight?

Jason wasn't in bed with her. He hated sleeping next to her when she'd been drinking. Neither she nor he had drawn the curtains the night before, and behind the big-leafed houseplant they'd bought when first moving in together she could see the wall of the red-brick factory that had recently been converted to condos. A bus lumbered past. After the noise receded she heard pigeons burbling outside on the window ledge and saw the tops of three slate-colored heads at the bottom of the pane.

On the wall next to the window was the bird her Finnish grandmother had given her on the trip to Europe. It was a kind of folk-art emblem fashioned on a flat piece of wood, three inches tall and two wide, with a drawing in black paint of a sideways bird, its beak turned toward its tail, as if it were looking back toward where it had come from. *Sielulintu*, the artist had written on the back, and she had looked up the meaning later. It meant soul-bird. In Karelian mythology, it was a bird you gave to newborns to deliver their soul to them, and when you died, the soul-bird carried it away for you. In very old times, they would bury a dead child with a tiny finch in her mouth, to take her onward to wherever she was going.

As Kate looked at it, she remembered her grandmother pressing it into her hands whilst nodding and scrunching her wrinkled eyelids and in every other way trying to convey to her the significance of that moment in both their lives.

She tried to get up, but as s soon as she lifted her head an astounding scythe of pain sliced across it. Now that she was aware of it, she felt the ache revolving slowly inside her skull, round and round, an excruciating rotation, at the speed of a cement mixer.

She staggered to the bathroom for painkillers and heard the TV on low volume and Jason breathing heavily on the couch. In the bathroom mirror her eyes stared back huge out of her drawn face, in a hungover illusion of dehydrated beauty.

Back in bed she took pill after pill to combat the pain, seven in all—three at first, then two, and two more, at half-hour intervals, but the pain didn't ease. Jason was moving around now, she smelled coffee, heard him clattering and doing dishes and bagging recycling. She felt her heart rustle within its cavity and wondered how much wine she had drunk on top of the champagne. Her heart beats were too shallow, like whipped sugar. And it was strange—she thought she sensed a trace of post-sex languor under her ribcage, a sweet sticky feeling in her hips and thighs that as not from the "shag" with Jason. Maybe she'd had a steamy dream. She tried to see past the headache and the white light of inebriation...

A flash of something, a shadow, flipped past.

She thought to check between her legs for clues, for telltale signs of sex. That's when she became aware that she couldn't move. Her hand and arm simply did not budge. At the same time, she felt herself being filled with an infusion of lust. There was no mistaking the feeling, it was familiar and delicious. She thought: let go, why don't you? The feeling swelled, she was cloud-like, porous and light. *Let go, let yourself fly!* Something about the lightness was terrifying. She shook off the feeling, wriggled her legs and mashed the back of her head against the pillow. She could move again and placed her hand gently on her pubis and felt herself seal shut like an envelope.

Jason called to her, he wanted to go out for bagels, and somehow she managed to get out of bed and stand even though her body was screaming *don't get up, it is imperative to stay put!* She opened her mouth to say, "I think I'm going to fall" but nothing came out and she fell onto her knees between the bed and the window, grasping for something and bringing down the houseplant, and it really was very much like what Alice experienced on the way to Wonderland, except that she didn't see any chairs or teapots, only a neon-thought flashing in front of her as she plunged, on-off, on-off, like an advertisement. Don't do it, it flashed, Don't do it to Terrance, Don't die, DON'T DO IT.

She went through the black hole.

The next thing she knew was that she was able to stand again. Jason got her dressed, and they walked down to the hospital, six blocks away. "You're OK," he kept saying. "It was only a minute or two. After you fell."

In the emergency room, she sat bent over next to him, gazing at the waxed, grey linoleum. It was as if gravity had risen from below and climbed to sit on top of her shoulders, the weight pressing her down into the ground, but where the ground was supposed to be was only air.

They put her on a gurney and carted her to a curtained-off exam area, Jason holding her hand all the way. The room hummed with equipment and air conditioning. The mattress was cold and hard.

A grey-beard neurologist came in and asked if she had experienced trauma to her head, while a nurse took her blood pressure.

"No," Jason said.

The doctor shone a light into Kate's eyes. "Do you know where you are?"

A woman on the other side of the white curtain moaned plaintively, like a lone bird on a remote islet. Kate turned toward the sound and said to her: I fell through a mirror into a big black hole. I'm not quite sure who I am right now. I'm Kate, yet not-Kate. I'm Kate-ish.

"Can you tell me your name, dear?" The nurse had positioned herself at the foot of the gurney and looked at her penetratingly. "What year is it, can you tell me?"

My name is Katarina…it was in—the year, the year of… what had she asked?

She understood from the nurse's bland expression that she wasn't hearing her words. The words weren't coming out. She tried harder. "Katarina."

"Kate," Jason said.

"Can you feel this, Kate?" The nurse was pinching her toe.

Katarina. She was remembering something, it was coming out, bubbling inside her.

"Send her for a CT scan." The doctor turned to her. "You're a nice girl, Kate, you'll be fine, don't you worry."

I'm thirty-nine, you fucker, she thought, but couldn't say. Under the neon tubes in the ceiling the doctor's face reverberated and the light kept leaning on her head, pushing her down.

The next time she opened her eyes Jason was asleep in a

chair next to the gurney. "Hey," she said.

Jason's face came alive. "Babe, how are you feeling?"

"What time is it?"

"Eight in the morning."

"I have to call work."

"You won't be working for a while, missus." Jason seemed almost satisfied. "You've had a little baby stroke. But you'll be ok and I will take care of you while you get better."

Behind the curtain the woman from earlier complained hoarsely, wordlessly. Her Finnish grandmother had sounded like that when she was dying at the hospital in Finland, when her uncle patched them in from the hospital room so they could be part of the experience.

Kate closed her eyes, remembered the clasp of her grandmother's rough hands. She felt quite safe as her mind carried her out to sea, past smooth hunks in a wonderfully silent sea, like what she had seen in Finland. No seagulls even. She floated in the boundless, barren void. Maybe she could drift a little farther still?

—

On her first day back home she lay on the couch in the living room, with its smell of bygone familiarity. Outside, the breeze sent last year's leaves and scraps of food wrappers tumbling along the sidewalk, she could hear their gentle scratch against concrete. She knew Jason could hear them too.

"You should go to work," she said.

"But are you ok? I was going to take the day—"

"No, go."

All summer, from marigold mornings to slowly steeping evenings she watched the shadow of the tree outside their window creep along the wall, passing over the Bulova clock that hung above the table. They hadn't changed the battery, and the clock's minute-hand set back tiny increments of time. Mornings, in the kitchen, she leaned against the counter feeling the rumble of the F train underneath the apartment building, listening to the death rattle of the coffeemaker. As long as the edge of the counter bit into her hip she could keep standing. There was no question of work. As soon as she sat at a computer, the world tumbled. Her vision vibrated, and certain colors created surreal effects. Pink, for example, so that when she looked at a pink object, it dyed whatever was beneath it a sickly, poison green. At night, even in the densest dark, she saw twinkling stars and flares like northern lights.

She had lost the art of small talk entirely. Solemnly, humorlessly, she uttered trivialities and spoke only when spoken to. Being asked questions was the worst, like having her tongue covered in Saran wrap. When the agency called again, she let the machine pick up. Finally the managing director left a message to say they had paid her for her one week of unused vacation time, "as a courtesy." No more P.S. Kate. She never wore the breast button anymore.

While Jason worked, Terrance and Gianna checked on her and brought food and ran errands. "How are you, Rina," Terrance asked sometimes and seemed to look at her meaningfully.

"You and Jason are so perfect for each other," Gianna told her one day when she brought down a tuna casserole. The implication, Kate supposed, was that the 'perfection' was a result of her and Jason's respective disabilities. She scraped the casserole into the trash and left the dish in the hallway outside the door.

After that, only Terrance came. One night, after handing her the to-go bag from the deli, he sat down next to her on the couch. On the kitchen radio, Jason's voice promoted his new morning show, his accent as big and ranging as a rancher's. "Rina." Terrance's voice was almost too soft to hear. "Do you remember the party at all, on your birthday?"

"Yeah. Sure. Why?"

He kept looking at her until she had to get up, to avoid the unpleasant feeling of confusion.

"Never mind," he said.

She was relieved when he left.

—

Jason texted from the F train. She was to meet him on 7th Avenue in ten minutes.

He came running up the subway stairs, talking into his phone and passing slower commuters. "Kate?" He stopped at the top of the stairs.

"Over here."

He brushed her shoulder and gestured toward the park, one block up the hill, continuing his conversation all the way through the entrance and down the walkway to the artificial lake. It was early October and dusk, and some of the trees across the lake had already turned.

They stood next to each other, she looking out across the lake and he cradling his phone. She blinked. It was hard to keep a whole scene together now—she could no longer see both the trees and the sky, only one or the other. Whenever she tried to take in the whole, the scene shuddered, as if it were about to come apart. She drew a breath, about to explain this to Jason, but he put a finger on her lips and smiled. "On hold," he whispered to her and kept his finger pressed to her lips. She smelled gun oil.

She flicked the tip of her tongue against her teeth and imagined the lightness of a bird in her mouth.

Jason let go of her. *Sielulintu*, she whispered to herself as he returned to the call, pounding the earth with the toe of his shoe for emphasis while he talked, his back toward her now.

With this thing that had happened to her head, it was as if her ability to feel anything for other people had been suctioned clean out of her, and she couldn't remember if this—this nothing-feeling—was how she'd felt about Jason all along.

She wandered over to a big poplar. It was one in a crescent of old trees along the waterline, where she used to jog in hot weather, crossing from one pool of tree shadow to the next, seeking shelter from the sun.

In the tree's shadow, under its red and orange foliage, she felt as if she had stepped into the shadows that had followed her all her life—and while Jason, as usual, was in the sun, his face tilted toward it, she was in this other place where light didn't reach.

A few seed balls of late-season dandelions bobbed in the breeze. She had no one to pick dandelions with, no one to blow the seeds into the wind with.

Once, she had walked in a whole field of dandelions, in Finland or in Latvia. She remembered the air thick with their spores, and suddenly, with the new clarity, remembered it crystal-clear, how the blade of the neighbor's circular saw had flashed in the air after it sliced through the hawthorn, and how right before that, she had been staring at her grandmother's garden swing, at the worn spot in the center of it, where her grandmother had sat all those years that they hadn't known each other—a whole life of dandelions taken from them both. The realization she'd had in that moment wasn't only that life was uncontrollable but that there was a whole dimension of life that she had no knowledge of, except that it was there. It was missing from the orderly suburban life her parents had made in New Jersey, missing from her buzzy friendships in high school. She hadn't found it in college, or in her film studies, not even in love.

It would have been better if her parents had never taken her on that trip, if she had never seen her "roots". The trip had only added to the gaps and the voids that were already in her and underlined the missing words on her tongue.

She looked toward the artificial lake, and the setting sun, and Jason, and the more she tried to focus on his outline against the copper sky, the more he vibrated, as though he were crackling at the edges, as though he were electrified. She was outside of it all, on her own, an afterthought.

THE GHOSTS OF
OTHER IMMMIGRANTS

ON THAT LAST NIGHT AT THE CORNER BAR, she says she likes to
listen to a) Frank Sinatra and b) Ingrid Caven singing French
chansons in German, not necessarily in that order.

Oooh, that voice, Ingrid *Caven*!

Her own squeaks with excitement and she looks askance in
coy horror. It was a beautiful cabaret voice once, hers, she says with
a theatrical bend of the wrist, and purses her rose lips around the
cocktail straw.

Latvian, eighty-five (she let it slip), with painted-on
eyebrows, a powdered face and whippoorwill hair under a black
beret, it's all softness about her—the silk bow at her throat, the
elegant fabrics, the frothy highballs with forgotten names. It's
unclear what *hers* is—Dagnica, Dana, Leigh—she claims them
all, and the professions of actress, callgirl, singer. Her gestures are
a comedy of manners, and she tells stories of high drama, of the
singing career, before her voice was ruined, of nights in New York,
of lovers, of women and men.

She is losing her friends and her memories, and we remind
her of her preferred ones, to let her shine. She knows: a shrewd
appreciation in her eyes.

Tell us about Latvia, when you were little.

She laughs a stage laugh, though it tinkles.

The parties, oh! and the Latvian traditions! The porch, and

the cherry trees…my mother, she had such deep kind of carpentry, so pale, I don't know how she kept those carpets clean.

Dagnica/Dana/Leigh, confusing carpentry for carpetry, in the house the Russians stole, so many decades ago.

I had a white dress...

When you were little? I ask, imagining a flapper frock and an oversized bow on her head.

…*you don't need a house* they said to me, they gave it to my brother and gave me two thousand dollars. *You'll get married,* they said. But I never did.

You mean the house in Latvia?

In New *Jersey*! I had to get out, I was under terrible stress, and he stole everything, all the porcelain and the lace.

I thought it was the Russians who stole—

An angry pivot of her head. Her eyes glitter cold.

Those damn Russians!

Oh, no, tell us about the men, about love.

Oh! There were so many, artists, you know, painters, handsome, they painted pictures of me, so many, all over the walls.

I had once visited her Ninth Street tenement where we sat in her kitchen drinking green highballs while a rat emerged from behind the refrigerator. She had measured me: would I scream—I dare you, her eyes said. I didn't, nodded only and drank the sweet liquor and picked up my bag as the rat bustled, unconcerned by our presence. We shared a jar of Swedish herring and Russian black bread even though the Swedes had once owned Finland and the Russians us both. Afterwards she led me through her two runty rooms, in the first a twin-sized bed of cloudy linens and ruched satin pillows, in the second a bay window coated with decades of dust. In the filtered light, the walls of the room sighed with fading portraits of a nude with easy contours: bare young flesh in oil, watercolor and Kodak, just as she had told us, rendered by artists content to replicate her perfect breasts with little heed to the complications of their subject. Otto Dix or Alice Neel might have perceived more, but they hadn't come knocking.

Now, the beret slips. She's on her second cocktail.

Tell us about the teleprompters, someone says.

Oh, the teleprompters, they call me all the time, every day, trying to sell me things!

Her voice shrills, gets away from her, and she sighs.

I was going to the burial.

Oh, did someone die?

…he was an Italian, they put him on that island with the prisoners, it's on the subway map. No, you can't go, the woman says to me—there's no funeral for destitutes. She said he was a destitute.

She's talking about the potter's field on Hart Island, run by Rikers inmates. She rounds her eyes as if to focus.

I have cadillacs, in my eyes.

Cataracts?

Yes, like I said!

The corners of her mouth turn, and like a child in a grown-up's chair, she treads her feet in the air.

You should fix your hair nicer, she says to me, the way my grandmother in Finland used to, and digs out her money purse. She's had her fill of gimlet and us.

Better leave in fair weather, she says.

Better leave before her bowlegs fail again on Second Avenue and leave her leaning on a lamp post in the rain.

Good night, she says, is helped down from her stool.

See you soon, I say.

She kisses me on the mouth, a powdery taunt.

Maybe you will, she says, her eyes in flinty slits, and maybe you won't, and I think that in a few short decades this is me, this shrunken woman bent over a cane, a long way from home.

CALDERAS

ON THE FIRST MORNING IN THE AZORES, she opened the kitchen window of her Ponta Delgada apartment rental onto a lush, overgrown backyard, where a brown cat was stepping gingerly over clumps of dead vine draped over a stone wall.

Funny how cats were the same the world over—this Portuguese cat could just as well have been a Brooklyn cat. It made its way toward another cat, perched on the roof of a water-logged shed underneath an abundantly flowering tree. A third, a black-and-white tom, was lying half-concealed amongst a neighbor's pastel-colored sheets drying in the misty air. She craned her neck to get a better look at the house next door to hers, and there spied yet another cat, asleep under the eaves of what appeared to be an abandoned building. It was the same shade of orange as Tasket, the cat she had given up to be with Dix, who was allergic. For years afterwards, Tasket appeared to her in dreams, and knew how to talk.

The orange cat was so close that she could have reached out and touched it. She aimed her phone at the composition of mossy beam with orange cat. At the sound of the shutter, the animal opened its green eyes and regarded her, offended.

The night before, it had taken her more than an hour's wandering through a maze of dark and deserted streets, narrow as corridors, to find the house. Each historic block turned out to have its own name, and to her, still on Eastern Standard Time and dragging a suitcase across the wet cobblestones, São Francisco Xavier, Campo de São Francisco, R. João Francisco Cabralin and Rua D. João Francisco de Sousa all seemed like "that street with 'Francisco' in it" that she had scribbled onto a post-it note at the office.

She recalled the images of the mythical-seeming Portuguese islands that had spurred her to take this trip and found nothing 'exotic' in the heavy gray bulging down from the sky.

—

When the plane had taken off from Boston to Ponta Delgada, after the short flight from New York, she prayed for the second time that day that the plane would arrive safely in its destination. She did not believe in prayer but as a child had developed this annoying tick that required her to link her fingers and mental-mumble incantations about a safe landing whenever she flew.

The flight was smooth and uneventful, leaving her free to indulge in revelry about the upcoming three weeks—just her, no office, no plans, no bad history. She was fit, strong, ready for adventure after months of going to the gym during her lunch hour. She was not—she repeated to herself, not—the kind of person who was going to let a broken heart get in her way. She was fine, she was fantastic, traveling alone to a strange, new, exotic place, not as a tourist but as a wanderer on the crust of the earth; to a place comfortably removed from the landmasses of America and Ireland, both of which she and Dix had lived in during their fifteen years together; to a place entirely untouched by that previous life, and she could maybe finally forget about the breakup, about almost jumping off the roof of their building, about the months of despair, about Dix's pregnancy.

The Portuguese islands were suspended vertically between

Greenland and Antarctica, two mythical continents that she would never visit, and near Africa where she had never been. She turned pictures of the green mountains and blue lagoons of the Azorean calderas into her screensaver at work, and in November when Dix emailed to tell her about the pregnancy ("I wanted you to hear it from *me*"), she had set the screensaver to start every five minutes, so that each time she returned to her desktop she was met with the stunning volcanic lakes.

Somewhere over the Atlantic she tore out an ad from the airline magazine, for a tour company offering "action-packed immersion adventures." The ripping sound woke up the toddler next to her, and his crying in turn awakened two other babies, one in front of her and the other across the aisle, the three of them forming a Bermuda's triangle of wailing as they competed for prominence on the small craft. As with dogs in the night, when the crying of one began to wane, another baby picked up the slack, all the way from the wide-open seas to touchdown on São Miguel Island. But even this could not dampen her mood, and as she watched the islands slowly rise from the sea, she was so excited that her whole body was buzzing.

—

Out on the street after breakfast, she inspected the abandoned house next door.

There had been a business of some sort on the ground level. Through the display window she saw that the building was completely ruined, overtaken by rain and moss—all of it: filing cabinets, office chairs, water-cooler, all coated with a perfect, velvety green. In Brooklyn, this could have been an art installation. She wanted to snap a picture of it, but even though there was no one else in sight, standing in the quiet street cellphone in hand felt like blowing a trumpet to announce "Tourist!"

Despite the lack of other pedestrians, the morning traffic was heavy and she had to keep flattening herself against the houses in the narrow streets whenever a car approached. Everything seemed to have been made for smaller people, and her hip and elbows were constantly bumping against the plaster walls as she walked toward the Europa Hotel, where the tour company was to pick her up. On the phone, the Portuguese-accented woman had told her that she had two options: an all-day sightseeing tour of the island or a four-hour hiking tour of Sete Cidades. The choice was obvious.

A few blocks before the hotel, she came across an old woman standing on a busy street corner, a cluster of plastic shopping bags at her feet.

'Delgada' in Portuguese meant tall, slender—she had looked up the word on her office computer—and this woman was tall, lanky, her long white hair and grey trench coat whipping in the Atlantic wind.

Over the zipping traffic, the woman locked eyes with her and called out in apparent alarm. Did she need help with her bags? She mimed an offer to carry them and help the woman across the road.

The woman lit up into a wide, glittering smile and shook her head.

The smile reached all the way inside her and sent chills through her body. It had been such a long time since she had felt anything so pleasurable in the months since the breakup; she had gotten used to walking around top-heavy with pain, like a clogged-up hourglass that never emptied.

When the light changed and the traffic stopped, she crossed to the other side, where the woman was talking animatedly, laughing and gesticulating. She could offer only helpless snippets of English in response to the woman's profuse Portuguese, the two of them seeking understanding and giving up with alternating shrugs and laughter, the useless words falling into the cobblestones.

Finally she turned to walk away but kept looking back over her shoulder at the old woman who was still standing there, smiling and waving. In the musty morning, her joy was like a bolt of lightning. How was such unbounded joy even possible?

A worker standing on a construction heap stopped shoveling when he saw her. "Guten Tag," he said, not at all welcomingly.

In New York, too, she was always being mistaken for German. She rounded the corner to the Europa where a young man was smoking outside. His beige hoodie was imprinted with 'Da Hood' across the back in jagged, faux-graffiti lettering. Behind him, a middle-aged woman with thin, shoulder-length hair dyed wine-red appeared through the sliding doors. She remained standing in front of the doors which kept sliding open and shut behind her.

She evaluated the woman for the likelihood of her being one of the hikers on the Sete Cidades tour: practical shoes, loose khakis, sports jacket and backpack. Not a pro hiking outfit like hers, but passable for a tourist. "Are you here for the pickup," she asked the woman in English.

The woman waved her hands passionately. "No, no, no."

She wasn't sure if it was "no, I am not" or "no, no, I don't speak English."

A second woman, then a third, came out and the four Germans—they turned out to be part of the same group—all began to chat.

When the van appeared, she made for the rear seat next to the window, in the farthest corner of the last of the three rows.

"Oo, sie hoppt!" the second German woman said to her, halting her own effort to board the van to indicate with her hands how she had "hopped" into the van. The woman was older and shorter than the wine-haired one, with lipstick the color of fresh brick and hair tinted a bland yet distinct brown. "Dieser Van ist nicht für kurze Leute," she said, issuing a thin giggle and joining her in the back seat.

Kurze Leute. Short people. Her college German from twenty-five years earlier was enough to understand most of what the woman said in her high, watery voice—if Billie Holiday sang molasses, this woman spoke cooler condensate. How on earth would Kurze Leute hike a caldera if she had trouble getting into a van?

The wine-haired woman also sat in the backseat while Da Hood and his girlfriend sat behind the driver and the guide. The van started off and the skinny guide began in German.

After a while, when no English seemed forthcoming, she interrupted in English. "Excuse me, is this going to be all in German?"

The guide and the driver, a stocky crew-cut man in his thirties, exchanged a look. "You do not speak German?" He gestured toward the driver. "So he will speak English, and I will translate in German if necessary."

For the second time that day someone had taken her for a German. Hardly able to hear the driver's stream of English, spoken at the windshield in a surprisingly American accent, she settled in to examine the landscape as the others chatted, freed from listening duty by the English-language narration. A few times she discerned the words "Sete Cidades," and the satisfying sense of anticipation about to be fulfilled grew inside her. Even if the volcanic lakes were only a quarter as beautiful as in the photographs, and even if she had to hike in the company of these tourists, it would be worth the day trip.

The abundance of green slathered over the passing hills struck her as familiar somehow: the neatly sectioned fields, black-and-white cows in pastures, stone fences garlanded with vines and roses…She attempted to reject the insight, but it was all too obviously reminiscent of the Irish countryside.

On nearly every house, on tiles from oval to oblong, was a depiction of the Blessed Virgin Mary. Of all the 'tropical,' 'exotic' places in the world, she had chosen an island in the Atlantic dominated by cow pastures and Catholicism.

—

At a tea plantation, in the midst of some rolling hills, during a prolonged and uneventful inspection of the machines for processing tea, she left the group to wait outside and found the driver smoking. He indicated the even rows of squat shrubs. "This tea plantation is very important to São Miguel Island. Not as important as it used to be, but still very important."

"How long will we be here?" She knew that all the sightseeing on the way to Sete Cidades was a bonus, but she was impatient to get on with it.

The driver cocked his head. "Where is your accent from? You are Canadian?"

She had spent her college years tenderizing her Finnish-inflected Northern Michigan accent into the closest possible approximation of a generic American drawl, but after she and Dix had moved in together, the accent she had fostered had begun to acquire the lilts and twists and whistling, flute-like cadences of Dix's Irish English. No matter how she tried, traces of the changed accent clung to her words, like fungus, and her mind still teemed with words like gobsmacked, laddie-o, missus, wanker, wallop…

After the tea tour, the driver raised his voice in the van, in English: "The area we are passing through now was the most important agricultural area on the island in the 18th century. Also," he held up his forefinger, "this is the flattest agricultural area of the island, and therefore one of the most important."

"Ja, ja," said Da Hood's girlfriend and giggled.

The van charged up a steeper hill. "On the right, you will see the village of Furnas, but we will first go to the top of the caldera."

Was this Sete Cidades already? She began to lace up the

hiking boots she had loosened during the drive and drank some bottled water to hydrate.

"Ui-ui," said Kurze Leute, when the van narrowly passed another great white van racing down the hill.

Up top, they beheld a view of a village, a lake, and what the driver called "a dry lake"—a flat area of green. Not Sete Cidades. "In Portuguese," the driver said to her, correctly identifying her as the only one who might care, "a 'caldeira' means any hot hole in the ground. In English, 'caldera' is the whole thing." He swung his arm to indicate the rim of the volcano, then boomed to the rest of the group: "This is the only place where you can see ALL of them—the village and the lake and the dry lake—when you are in one, you cannot see the other."

She failed to understand the significance of his statement. Still, the landscape was beautiful, less like Ireland and more like what she had come for, and it made her look forward to Sete Cidades all the more.

—

Down in the village they walked around a belching hot spring in the middle of a rocky plateau. She thought of the man in America who had fallen into a hot spring in a national park shortly before her trip. He had died immediately, the authorities said, but before his body could be recovered, it had dissolved in the hot water. Boiled.

Jumping up and down to get her blood flowing, she calculated how much time would be left over for hiking. Maybe the idea was that they would drive straight back afterwards—it wasn't far, and there were still hours and hours left of the day.

The area of the hot springs was furnished with Biblical stand-up figures of herders, goats, and women bearing earthen water jugs—it was as if the whole world had been shrunk down to a theme park of totems of her life with Dix: the orange cat that morning, the Catholic figures, the cultural chasm between her and the driver, and between her and the other tourists, even her presence on the tour—a tour she should have never been on.

She tried to recollect the word for Christian scenes being displayed together like this; the years with Dix had given her a general cultural sense of Catholicism, but the technicalities still evaded her. "Does 'Furnas' mean something?" she asked the driver, who was yawning.

"'Furna' in Portuguese is something like a hole inside the ground. In English, there is only one word—'hot springs'—but in Portuguese, we have two words: for the springs where the water is bubbling and for the springs where the water is just hot."

She inquired about the walking part of the tour, avoiding the word 'hiking' because maybe it was she who had misunderstood the nature of the tour. Perhaps something had been lost in translation and it would be more of a 'walk.'

"There will be some walking later, in the park."

The park. This was really just a sightseeing tour. She hated sightseeing tours, so much so in fact that she had never been on one before. She could have seen the cow-studded countryside on her own, or stayed behind to make friends with townspeople like the old woman, whose smile still shone in her mind.

The driver stopped at a tap protruding from rock. "Spring water. Cold." He filled a plastic water bottle and took a swig.

She emptied out the spring water she had bought at the airport and replaced it with this new water.

It tasted horrible. She stifled her grimace—maybe people got used to their water, as they did to their air. The driver might not like the tap water in New York.

They repeated the same ritual at a second faucet. The water was only slightly less horrible. "It's sweeter," she said as the driver stared, and she wondered if she'd be able to get the whiff of Furnas out of the plastic.

No one else tasted the water. Later, the Germans would probably get together at the hotel bar to laugh at the dour "Amerikanerin" who had imbibed the disgusting dribble.

—

Stations of the Cross, it came to her at the lake, when she saw ducks and geese congregating around a hut that dispensed birdfeed and human snacks. Tour guides greeted each other grimly amid the tourists flocking toward a roped area where heaps of ashy soil resembling ants' nests were spaced a dozen feet apart.

She gazed longingly at the surrounding hills and the steep rock face leading up to a spear-shaped peak at least twenty stories high. Where she wanted to be.

Two men holding long sticks with hooks approached one of the ashy heaps. Clearing the top with his boot, one of them used the stick to pluck off a wooden lid covering—what else—a hole in the ground. In it was a large stainless-steel pot. The men lifted the cauldron into the air, pausing for photographs like socialites at a Manhattan cocktail party. Camera shutters chattered as they walked off with the pot, and a grey-bearded man followed them with a camcorder.

The driver found her and continued to speak rapid Portuguese into his cellphone. "What is your room number?"

"I don't have a room number, I'm staying at an Airbnb."

"But you are part of the reservation that was made by the German group..."

Did he still think she was German? "No, I made my reservation this morning."

"I think I see what happened," the driver said and walked away.

What happened, she wondered in the van as they followed a narrow lane that could have been in County Cork. At a fork in the road, a mustachioed man in grey lederhosen sat on a log, lunching on a sandwich wrapped in wax paper.

"Whooo, ui-ui, er sitzt da," Kurze Leute said.

The driver looked over his shoulder. "The restaurant where we will eat in Furnas…"

They were going back to Furnas? Was there nowhere else to eat before Sete Cidades?

The driver and guide abandoned all pretense of guiding the tour and launched into a long exchange in Portuguese, punctuated by laughter, while the rest of them sank into the apathy of outsidership.

Back in the village they were led into a cold, tiled dining hall with tables pre-set for large groups. As soon as they sat down, two platters stacked with pink, red, brown and beige lumps of meat—pig, blood sausage, beef-something, chicken—and discolored hunks of potato were brought to the table by stolid-faced young men in national costume. A heavy meal—too heavy. Suddenly she realized there would be no Sete Cidades.

"I'm sorry there was a mistake," the driver said next to her, as though he had read her mind.

"Oh, it's ok, I mean, it's enjoyable anyway." It wasn't!

"If you want, you can pay for another tour, a hiking tour, later."

"Pay? But this isn't the tour I was supposed to be on."

"You came, you have to pay—but you get discount. This tour is seventy euros, but you will get it for the fifty that you paid. This is longer. If you want another tour, you have to pay for it."

"But this is not what I ordered," she said, sounding so American. She examined the food, too hungry not to eat something. On the edge of one of the platters, a small area was taken up by cabbage—"boiled to slobber" was how Dix would have described it. A few slivers of carrot lay limp against the cabbage. She took some, along with a drooping fold of cabbage, and after hesitating, speared a child-size section of chicken.

During the meal she left to use the restroom. There, a middle-aged woman was measuring her mother's blood sugar. The older woman looked so much like Dix's that she was startled when she spoke in Portuguese.

In the stall, she formulated the arguments that had evaded her during the confrontation with the driver. "If you order a hamburger and get a tuna sandwich, you don't have to pay for it." Or, "If you order a bra and get a pair of socks, you don't have to pay for it—you simply return the incorrect item and get your money back, or exchange it for the correct one." Or, if one part of a couple cheats on the other, the cheater is the one who must move out, unlike what had happened with Dix.

Instead of returning to the dining hall she went outside to look at the little town, perched on a hillcrest, the houses jutting helter-skelter along winding roads, their windows like dead eyes seemingly alive to everything outside whilst keeping secret whatever they held inside. Just like towns she had seen in Ireland, with women tarrying in front of their houses, pretending to sweep while keeping an eye out.

She heard the sound of hooves on pavement and turned to see a goat cantering toward her, and two men in chase. The animal faltered when it saw her and veered off-road, toward an enclosure that ended in a gate—an impasse. All three, the men and the goat, turned to stare at her. I'm not German, she thought.

—

"The park" was an overgrown botanic garden with a pool of brown water at the center. The water was the color of old-lady nylons, and people were floating in it.

The driver looked at his watch. "We will meet at 4:10. Enjoy the water."

More than an hour and fifteen minutes away. "For fuck's sakes," she said out loud. There was no way she was removing her clothes in this cold, sad arboretum, with these people.

She took off down a stone path. Judging from the map on the brochure, the walk around the park was a long one, although the map did not indicate how long. She walked briskly to make sure she returned on time, barging past the few visitors she encountered on the pathway, lined with dense, tall cane on one side and dark woods on the other.

There was no discernible scent to the arboretum, only the mugginess that was closer to a physical presence than a smell. It was so damp that on the fluff of her sweater, the moisture from the air was gathering into microscopic pearls of dew. She maintained a rapid pace until, after about fifteen minutes, the white building that overlooked the dirty pool reappeared. She had gone around the entire park.

She sat down on one of the benches encircling the pool. Waiting, again. Why was she always waiting, as if her real life were taking place somewhere else, some place she had to hurry toward, instead of being *here*. Maybe she was the problem. She examined her flaking nails—it was so humid that even her nail fungus, normally under control, had reactivated. She was becoming part of the damp of this island in the middle of the Atlantic. It seemed as if at any moment, the humidity might tip past the critical point and turn everything into a stew of rot, her along with it.

With her cellphone, she began to take extreme close-ups of the wet, mossy, lichen- and algae-covered surfaces, to document the miserable damp. An Irish damp—the green-turning-to-black parks, the slippery stone pavements, the moss-covered mounds, women who aged like Dix's mother...*It's in emergencies and difficulties souls are made*—the words in the book she had been reading on the plane came to her as she photographed, and something lurched in her stomach, as though she were standing over a precipice, about to fall. Or as though the heavy feeling in her head had slipped down to her abdomen.

A few feet away, the head of Kurze Leute bobbed past in the brown water. Her friend was there too, two inches of silver growth forming a sea anemone at the roots of her wine-colored hair.

She found the driver and guide loitering near the arboretum's wrought-iron gates. "You know, if you went to America," she told the driver, "no one would know you're not American." It was true, in his preppy polo shirt he looked more Irish American than anything else.

He was offended. "Really? No one has ever said that to me before."

"Yup, all-American. Like a football player."

—

Their final stop was a church on a hill, high up over the Atlantic on the southern shore.

The church was locked; they were only there for the view.

She walked back and forth in the parking lot, waiting for everyone to finish taking the requisite panorama shots of the ocean, which they had been photographing every chance they got. She stooped to pluck one of the fat pink blooms dropped by the same tree she had seen from the Airbnb and later in the arboretum.

The petals were staunch and thick and smelled of nothing. She thought of the lines of a Finnish poem she had translated in college. "Somewhere far away in a distant land / is a bluer sky and a stone wall wreathed in roses / or a palm tree and a softer wind / and that is all." She was Somewhere Far Away, and that was all; the flowers had no scent, and what of it.

At the base of the hill, below the church, four identical cats were slinking around each other, assembling near a hole in the hillside. As she watched, one crawled into the opening and settled on its haunches, its tail still outside, while its three siblings sat around regarding their sister. She had never seen a cat stick its head in a hole or any kind of enclosure—cats always mapped their escape. What kind of cat just sat there, its face deep in the dirt, its backside unprotected? It went completely counter to a cat's most basic instincts.

The feeling that emerged within her as she watched the cat with its arse sticking out of the church hill was: that was her, the way she had spent the last years with Dix, pretending things were fine, whereas things had not been fine. They had somehow managed to entertain each other for ten years, to fit each other's old, unmet needs with the other's traumas, and become locked solid into a dance across their thirties. She wondered if Tasket was still alive. He would be fourteen, past cat middle-age. There was nothing different, really, about the way she had discarded that cat to be with Dix compared to Dix dumping her to be with her new love.

Between the cats and a glass display depicting graphic scenes from the Bible was a set of rickety wooden steps half hidden in long grass and leading up the steep hill. She recognized only Jesus behind in the glass case—Jesus carrying the cross, toppled on the ground, conferring with a woman, and finally, resurrected, floating in the air as though filled with helium.

She glanced back at the tour group members beside the van, like hatchlings unwilling to leave their mother, and decided to risk the rickety stairs.

There was no banister. She felt her body shaking as she scrabbled up, half crawling, clutching the steps with her hands. The stairs ended on a grassy patch, on a kind of ledge that jutted out of the mountain, overlooking the church and the parking lot. Tufts of long grass and wildflowers frothed over the lip of the lookout, masking the sheer drop.

The space was barely big enough for two and secured with a low fence of slim, weathered beams that seemed no match for the 40-kilometer-per-hour gusts. It was a strange place to be permitted to trespass.

Her knees nearly buckling, the fear of falling threatening to morph into falling itself, she knelt on the ground and held on to the worn wood. This was not at all how she had felt up on the rooftop in Brooklyn, when she had believed she was ready to jump from their five-story apartment building—wanting—trying—leaning over the low edge, to put an end to the tearing pain, and as sick with the terror of what she was considering as with her inability to go through with it. Afterwards, she had returned to their top-floor apartment, right underneath the spot where she had just been crouching, and found Dix texting her new boyfriend, aglow with fresh love.

For as long as she lived she would not forget how she had walked down the leaf-strewn sidewalk in the cold March night, after Dix refused to let her stay, and looked up at the windows of their apartment for the last time, with no place to go.

She'd had to become so hard, to withstand it.

But she was feeling things now—like the ancient lava of a dry caldera beginning to spew, the pain was intent on getting out of her—and she realized that the problem was that she *wanted* to love those rolling hills and cow pastures and even the Mother Marys on people's houses—that she *did* love them, and had come to love many things Irish and Ireland—it was in her now, it was part of her.

She looked south over the Atlantic, toward Antarctica, more than 8,000 miles away, and imagined her anger-laced heartache, a thing separate from her like Jesus's bleeding heart, continuing to travel without her toward the bottom pole of the earth, where it would sink and shatter.

Beyond the green mountains, Ponta Delgada and the neon logos of its hotels and shopping centers were coming to life in the first thickening of dusk, and she imagined the white-haired woman from that morning in one of the narrow, sun-starved alleys beneath the lights, walking along a cobblestoned street, ready to smile at the next person she would meet.

With her back toward the great emptiness, she found the first rickety steps and began to make her way down, in her mind the image of the woman, alone, glorious, shining like a light.

YELLOWSTONE

1

As soon as I turned off the engine in the pitch black, I heard the toneless barking of a dog, twigs snapping as the animal rushed through the undergrowth. I waited until the barking receded before I got out and stepped onto the soft grass. There was a breeze on my face, damp and smelling of cold and void.

From memory I walked to where the footpath to the house began, the forest now silent. The dog might belong to a hare hunter; it was almost the season. I held out my hands toward the thicket of alder we had decided not to cut down that summer, to bar the occasional boater from witnessing our sunbathing and our nude meanderings from sauna to sea. My sandal landed on the rise of rock where the trail started, orienting me; I knew it as well as my own body: as a child I would run the fifteen or so yards with my eyes closed, bursting fast through the thicket to avoid ticks and mosquitoes.

Now, the sharp edges of alder leaves scratched my bare arms and cheeks. Before the airport, I had dressed for the heatwave I was anticipating in Brooklyn, though here in the south of Finland the August day had been cool. Up ahead I felt more than saw the dark hulk of the cottage and walked into the black enclosure of the covered porch. I paused to listen. No birdcalls, no one hammering end-of-season cottage repairs, no children squealing, no motorboats running, only the distant hum of the sea filling the air with a low-grade mutter, less a sound than a sensation, a presence.

The house key was where we always put it, inside the tool closet, under an overturned plastic ice-cream container hidden behind the bucket for picking blueberries. Chilly air from under the house rose up through the slits in the flooring, sparking my childhood fear of the murky crevasses upon which the cottage had been built.

Fumbling at the door I dropped the ringless key. My heart scraped a ragged claw across my chest. I knelt down, patting the planks, mindful of the quarter-inch slits between them. As a child I had been sent to crawl underneath the cottage to retrieve fallen items, the space too shallow for an adult. The thought of having to get down on my stomach in the dark to hunt for the tiny object amid dirt, insects, and possibly snakes nearly immobilized me. Then I felt the cold edge of the key against my right pinkie and levitated my hand above it, grasping it, careful as a surgeon.

Decades of familiarity guided the key to the lock in the heavy wooden door. The top hinge shrieked into the silence.

Inside, the silence had a different quality. I tried to turn on the light, but the room remained dark. I had left only that morning, but now the whole cottage had the feel of a place that had remained unvisited for centuries, like one of the period rooms we had strolled through at the Brooklyn Museum. *Boring*, you had said and walked on.

Was Brooklyn in the dark too? Surely the whole world couldn't be affected. Maybe it was only a Scandinavian phenomenon, an Icelandic volcano, not the dreaded and mythical one in Yellowstone. Probably, you were watching the local news in New York right now, listening to a NASA spokesperson explaining what had taken place on this side of the Atlantic, and how the situation might be resolved. I imagined your worry. I admit—I wanted you to worry.

I had been on my way to you, to convince you that it wasn't too late for us, unlike you had said just before you flew back home two days earlier. I wanted to tell you that we could still have children—yes, I was too old to get pregnant, but you weren't. I had driven to the airport early to return the rental car, impatient to get on with it all, when the darkness rolled in and the meticulous descent into chaos commenced. People began to drive back to their homes and loved ones like maniac robots. I looked at the advancing wall of black, incredulous that even catastrophes were stacked against me.

In the kitchen doorway the old flashlight hung from its hook. It was solid and heavy with big old-fashioned batteries and had a yellow beam that looked like a damaged retina if you shone it directly onto a smooth surface. When the beam flashed off the cupboard's glass door, it showed my own, ghoulish face, and I hastened to open the door, erase the image.

I checked for provisions. Before I left I had emptied the cabinets of anything that would spoil or go stale in the sea air. The remainder was a mix of new and ancient spice jars, flour, sugar, vegetable oil, vinegar, jasmine tea, and packets of instant soup. I had left the small refrigerator next to the cupboard running for my brother who would come for berry- and mushroom-picking weekends in the fall. Inside, the flashlight shone upon tonic water, ketchup, mustard, raspberry jam my aunt had made the year before, lingonberry jam, plus an unopened package of feta. The shoebox-sized freezer compartment was wet from melting ice and housed a half-drunk bottle of gin.

In the living room, the beam swept over the big round table and its eight chairs, where that summer we had sat with my family, looking out through the panoramic window that now faced the dimensionlessness outside. I turned off the flashlight. I could see a muted glow, a slight difference in the granulation of dark, indicating a wider space where normally I would see the black line of the horizon, the whiteheads tossing in the gap between the bay and the wide-open sea. Straining my eyes to our beach, I discerned a denser darkness in the shape of a triangle—the rowboat, face down on the rocks where it had lain all that summer, a fist-sized hole in the hull from when I took you rowing and kept watching you instead of the rocks submerged in the shallow water behind me.

2

WE HAD ALWAYS SAID TO ONE ANOTHER, staying up long, limpid summer nights, smoking cigarettes, and drinking warm beer, that if the world ended or a great catastrophe hit, we would come here to die. You and me and my brother, we had said it quietly, earnestly, letting long pauses expand between our words. *The last shore*, we said, savoring it, and gazed seaward over the stumps of alder that we had not spared. Every summer we cut them down. Every year they grew back to try and block our sunset view. They would have taken over our world if we hadn't stopped them with the weed whacker.

At the airport, making a U-turn on the access road and heading in the only direction where I could still see some light, back in the direction of the cottage, I had believed it was a temporary calamity, even though my cell phone wasn't working. Then the fires began. I don't know what started them—electrical shorts, some system-wide attack. I drove, calculating how far my dwindling gas would take me, and watched the flames crawl low through grass and moss, restrained because it had been a rainy summer. It had been beautiful, the crackling fire spreading slowly across the black landscape and golding everything in its path. I watched it lap at and devour fences and sheds and mailboxes, and almost stopped to take a picture on my phone. Maybe I could show you the photo someday, of this amazing thing I had experienced. But I could taste the smoke through the closed windows, and behind me in the rearview mirror the sky glowed red, so I had driven on in the only direction left.

The last sign I had seen of another human being was when I turned onto the dirt road after the village. There had been a light in a window of the farmhouse where we bought strawberries in the summer, where the cows came out to greet our car and peer at us with their huge frank eyes and plaster their meaty tongues against the dusty windows until whoever sold us strawberries shooed them back into their pasture. I had thought about stopping when I saw the solitary light in the darkness, but I didn't know him like that, and instead I turned my headlights off. After that, I didn't see anyone or anything, only the black, motionless forest, the rows of pine trunks stretching out to heaven like thin shadows as my Hertz hybrid heaved over the road's ruts and humps. Without the benefit of headlights it had felt like Space Mountain at Disney World: I had to give in and go with the motion of the road, letting its anatomy tell me where to go. It had taken a long time to clear the four miles to the cottage, and by then I had begun to worry that life as we'd known it was gone.

In the first dark days, the dog ran in a long, ranging loop for hours on end, from the ragged line of the seashore across the now-silent summer-cottage plots, through the still forest, round and round, acre after acre. Now I hear it less frequently. It never comes close enough for me to see it, but sometimes it stops running and I know it is sitting a short distance away, staring at me, smelling me. Then it tears back into the woods again.

I don't know how I have survived these endless days. I don't know how many there have been. Judging from the hot wave gripping my abdomen I am midway through my menstrual cycle again. My periods had already been waning, but I wonder if the absence of humans and pheromones will end them for good.

Surrounded by this black world, I would procreate with anything. What would it matter if it was a rabbit or a crazed dog, as long as life went on?

I think about you, about how you left me right at the moment of my loss of fertility. At first I believed it was a cruel coincidence, but now I realize it was the very thing, the reason why you wanted to go. You smelled in me the end of hope.

I can't see it, but I know the gap is out there, and beyond it the waves of the Gulf of Bothnia, then Stockholm, Copenhagen, New York, other shores where the sky might still be blue. Sometimes I wake to a hum and think the fires have found me, but it's always dark, nothing has changed. I dream of rain. It's only a matter of time before the fire catches up with me, I run out of things to eat, or some other misfortune befalls me. At least I have the well. Without it I would probably no longer be alive.

I found my father's stash of Russian cigarettes, from back when he still smoked, and I smoke them outside, even though there is no one to complain about smoking indoors. I sit on the wooden step beneath the birch tree's drooping branches, the leaves turning softer and flabbier by the hour. I pull them off one by one and rub them between my fingers, breathing in the pungent scent of life and the memory of summer saunas. I haven't heated the sauna; I can't sit in the warm, hissing cocoon, naked and unprotected and alone. When I light the match, the flame flutters over the birch leaves, some still flecked with tiny white dots of toothpaste, from tooth-brushing off the porch step all summer. A wild fear snaps at my lower abdomen as I smoke. I try to make myself calm down, to let the darkness in and be part of it, and crush the cigarette against a flat rock, carefully, reaching into the rainwater barrel to dribble water over the dregs of tobacco.

I wait. In the kitchen I keep the fire going. The irony does not escape me: as the world behind her burns to ash, the woman lights a fire. But I am cold, and the flames have not reached me yet.

I'm hungry. I pick blueberries, bog bilberries, black crowberries, eating them, making jam of the rest. They are already partially dried and rotted, or withered from the lack of sunlight. The muted sound they make when I drop them in the ice-cream bucket is hollow, inappropriate, ghostly. I pick lingonberries too, though they weren't ripe yet when the sun disappeared and are bone white on their belly side.

I stay close to the cottage. Behind me in the window, the faint warm glow of the stove latch. I turn away. The warmth is a cruel lie.

3

A TINY SPECK OF LIGHT crosses beyond the gap, and there is the thin roar of a faraway motorboat. It doesn't approach, probably fearing the rocky shoals. Only the thought of being lost alone in the wide-open sea seems more frightening than staying put. I don't know what to think of other people, I'm afraid to find them. What can you expect of people in this kind of situation?

I hear the dog, it's coming closer. Eventually it will lose its fear and approach me.

I go down to the shore finally, looking toward the bay. I haven't been all the way to the water's edge; I couldn't bear to face the tern-less, gull-less, spoonbill-less shore. I've heard a few little rustles, but no birdcalls, and I can't be sure it's birds making those sounds, not other animals. Maybe they flew away immediately, trying to outpace the dark. Maybe they knew before anyone else did.

What would the old folk have said of the smoke-tinged wind chopping at the black waves, would they have known its name?

Did this same kind of thing happen in other times, did people speak of it through generations until the knowledge was lost, or is this an entirely new thing, a one-time dying?

Following the contours of rock I find the boat. I glance over my shoulder at the house looming against the dark sky. Waves lap at the rocks a short distance away as I feel for the hole in the boat's hull. Maybe I could repair it. Go before others find me.

Every now and then I have checked to make sure the incongruous lump of the car is still there. It has a digital display with a clock and thermometer, and a Neverlost. Seeing the readings would require starting the engine, and the mere thought pitches me into a panic. The roar of the engine might tear apart whatever fragile remnant of reality remains.

I go back to the porch, light a match. I smell smoke in the air but don't know if it's my smoke or that of the rim of fire around me. I don't see it yet, but it must have already reached the village. I listen for the dog, which I still have not seen, listen for the lunatic barking and the thudding of frantic paws on dry earth, and catch a sensation of something rushing across the yard, so close I can smell its mad fear. In the momentary light from the match, a few meters away on a rock, a pair of eyes glints. It's not the dog though, the rock is along the hare's daily route, the rabbit we watched grow all summer from a tiny puffball into a strong, lanky adult. The rabbit is frozen in place and looks past me at something it probably can see as clearly as it sees me. Slowly, knowing I am no threat, it hops away. *I am not yet ready to eat you.*

The wind is rising. I don't know what it means. I pick berries, soon they will run out.

I fall asleep against the birch and dream of the sun. It shines from a strange angle. I'm at the bottom of a pond looking up at the sun shimmering through tawny water, out in a world that I can see but am not in. It is terrifying and beautiful.

SHE AND SIBELIUS

SHE STOPPED THE WHEELCHAIR in the middle of the living room and kept pressing the button on the remote so that Sibelius's *Symphony No. 5* ricocheted from every wall. The movement, with its unsettling haste and propulsion of emotion, had always been one of her favorites.

She closed her eyes and let the music carry her—like swimming, going fast, anticipating the swells—and when she felt them coming she whirled with the music, spiraling up, down, up, not knowing where, not caring.

But this time, even though the music was so loud that it rang across the length of the apartment, the sweet fullness of relief did not come. Without his presence back there in the kitchen, it all felt like nothing.

She opened her eyes in time to see a large white seagull flying past the window. The flash of its strong, smooth body only highlighted her feeling of separateness from the world outside. For the last five years, this room and its green tapestries, black-enameled piano and floor-to-ceiling wall of bookcases had been her refuge. She had needed the solitude, he had been so difficult after his stroke, tuning in and out of conversations and realities. *I'm trying to tell you what that girl did—pathological liar, hundred and sixty dollars, on lingerie!* He had said this about their daughter who wasn't even in Finland and whose retail spending habits, never mind lingerie purchases, he had zero knowledge of. He believed almost anything that anyone said, on the phone, in the newspaper, on television, twisting it and transposing it to make up his own nonsensical retellings in hours-long narrative collages that she could only escape by going to the living room and leaving him in the kitchen.

And now he was gone, slipped and fallen the way he used to joke it would happen, killed by the pair of wool socks she had knitted for his birthday.

"Murder socks," she said to the window where the seagull had been. The living room felt eerie, like visiting the past, or being a guest in her own home. Soon she would be talking to herself all day long, to be continued later in the hallways of whatever "home" they were putting her in as soon as a spot became available. As soon as someone else died and her name was next on the list. Her daughter, gone back to Michigan after his funeral, would return to manage the move, and she would become part of the legion of the drugged and dozing, twitching in their wheelchairs under the weight of their memories.

No one seemed to be concerned about the fact that she couldn't speak or really even understand much Finnish. It was he who had insisted they leave Southern Michigan and move to Finland, the country of his birth. She was American and had only been to Finland a handful of times despite her parents being first-generation Finnish. She was born and bred in New York, where her parents were buried, a stone's throw from the family mausoleum of their lifelong employer, on a Brooklyn hilltop. It was a prestigious cemetery, but her mother had been nanny to the youngest son who died in an accident at age four. He had been so devoted to his nanny that the family bought her and her husband a burial plot near theirs so their son would be near his beloved nanny forever.

Her own parents could have never afforded the plot—you didn't fare well in America if you spent your life working as a nanny and a handyman or, in her and her husband's case, cook and carpenter.

Now, with him gone, their forty years in Michigan seemed to have vanished, and she, the girl who left New York for the Midwest after falling in love with a Finnish carpenter, would never see America again.

She turned the wheelchair 180 degrees. The contrast between the cool exhumation on the back of her neck and the morning sunlight blazing in through the kitchen window functioned as a kind of wall that divided her life in two, giving her the sense of traveling from one place to another.

She entered the cone of light and rolled over the spot where he had fallen. She'd been in the living room when it happened and hadn't heard; it was only after the CD stopped spinning and she turned around that she saw his legs across the kitchen doorway, his feet in the grey wool socks.

The phone was in the kitchen—the center of their life, everything within arm's reach for cooking, eating and sleeping, plus the television, telephone and door buzzer—so she'd had to squeeze past him in the wheelchair to make the emergency call, but it was too late, she knew, feeling with the footrest of her chair how lifelessly his limbs reacted to being pushed aside.

His heart had been so weak he could barely stand for longer than a minute, but up until the end, his sliver of a body had continued to shuffle from stove to sink and sink to armchair and back, as he muttered about the price of cigarettes or some imaginary person or TV character—*she had this real attitude, this big thing*—on and on—*what you have to understand about these people*—she'd look up at him, not understanding and desperate for him to shut up, and he'd know and shout at her: *I'm talking about BLIND people!* And then his breathing would be so shallow it made her ache, and she really did wish she could understand.

She passed his old armchair, at the foot of the pullout bed.

"Where's that coffee," she said to the chair. "Do I have to make it myself?" She snorted, the phlegm in her throat stereoing the sound. He would have laughed first at the joke, then at her snorting. In between the monologues he could be good company, affectionate and full of laughter. "Ok, I'll make it myself."

Click-click, snap, a fine hiss, the gasp of the gas when she lit the flame like an intake of breath. Traffic sounds wafted in through the window. The squeal of brakes, the rumble of a passing streetcar, a distant ambulance. The harsh shreds of sound produced by groups of uproarious teens shouting at each other on their way to school.

She transported the coffee to the windowsill and swung the wheelchair around. In the old days, the wooden cover of the pullout bed had been opened only for overnight guests but for years now it had been *their* bed. The bed was about an inch too high for her—and had been too small for two, impossible to sleep wedged together, she had never slept properly with his body next to her, so hot.

In a radio documentary she had heard that Sibelius, too, had wanted to sleep separately from his wife, at least sometimes. Neither she nor Sibelius had ever managed it.

She hoisted herself up, arm muscles quivering from the effort, the sun on her neck heightening her frustration. Now she had the bed to herself. Her head against a heap of cushions from the living room couch she could see the television, on its shelf above the doorway. She had not switched it off since they'd carried him away, only muted the volume. Right now it was playing his favorite soap, the Spanish one she couldn't stand, with all the yelling. She had made him watch it with the earphones on.

The coffee was nowhere near as good as his.

On his more lucid days they had sometimes talked about how much longer they could endure this. They hadn't left the apartment except for a doctor's appointment for more than five years. The doctors had told them to stop drinking coffee and alcohol, mostly for his sake, but the regular home health aide had bought whatever they wanted. Now she had to endure two daily visits from a new girl who had refused to get her a fresh bottle of Cutty Sark, "for her own good."

She held up her mug and in her mind's eye toasted the entire school of "carers" who had banned everything that could momentarily lift the mind and body up from ache and degeneration. Restless legs, degeneration, knee surgeries, arrhythmia, and finally paralysis after that asshole rammed into her and her grocery bags with his what-car?—his ATV.

"An ATV—in the city!" She didn't care if the neighbor heard her, he could complain again if he wanted, about the music, about yelling. She remembered the tiny red winter apples she'd bought that day to make applesauce wobbling downhill across the intersection, and the smashed hull of the milk carton in front of her nose, the milk seeping into the cracks in the asphalt as she lay there, perplexed. The doctors had given her no hope of recovery.

Sometimes she daydreamed of being like the paralyzed man she'd once read about, thrown into a swimming pool by his neurologist, and how his first reflex in the situation had been to immediately begin to swim. Her reflex was that sometimes in the night she would kick involuntarily, which had made him bolt upright in the dark, grasping his chest, while she lay frozen and wondered whether this would be the thing that killed him.

Outside, clouds had moved in. Everything had gone gray. An explosion of laughter came from the all-day pub across the street, the drunks already settled in for a day of drinking and smoking under their orange awning. A streetcar rumbled up the hill.

The life, out there, like television life. Not her life.

A crash from the hallway. The mail—it always came after ten. In another hour, the home health aide would arrive for her first visit. Someone slammed a door.

In the living room, the Sibelius was reaching the end. Her eyes happened upon the stove and she noticed she'd left the knob slightly open, instead of lining up the little marks that showed that the gas was turned off. She pried herself up and lifted her withered legs over the edge, and the pillows broke formation behind her. The wheelchair seemed so far away. She shut her eyes, imagining she was on the edge of a swimming pool, and the world was wide open beneath her. She rocked her body from side to side and felt on her cheek the feathery touch of his fingers, the way he always stroked her first thing in the morning, and before sleep. An excruciating need shot through her, to feel the safety of him, his back against her breasts, her nose in the soft skin of his neck. She was light as a feather as she tipped over.

Outside, someone dropped a sheet of metal over the cobblestones and a jackhammer began. The pubgoers hollered in response.

ACKNOWLEDGEMENTS

"Monkey Bars"
Best New Writing, 2014. Editor's Choice Award

"1993"
The Iowa Review, 50:3 Winter 2020/2021.
Winner, 2020 Iowa Review Award in Fiction.
"Other Distinguished Stories of 2021" Honorable Mention in
The Best American Short Stories 2022

"Country Fiction"
Porter House Review, 2019. Nominated for a Pushcart Prize.

"The Ghosts of Other Immigrants"
*Short, Vigorous Roots: A Contemporary Flash Fiction Collection of
Migrant Voices*, Ooligan Press, 2022

"Yellowstone"
SAND Journal (Berlin), Summer 2018

Maija Mäkinen is a Finnish-born writer and translator whose work has appeared in *The Iowa Review*, *Porter House Review*, *The Bare Life Review*, *SAND*, and in the anthology *Short, Vigorous Roots – A Contemporary Flash Fiction Collection of Migrant Voices*. She has been awarded the University of Cambridge Lucy Cavendish Fiction Prize and the Nadia Christensen Prize in Translation, and residency fellowships to Art Omi, The Helene Wurlitzer Foundation, The Studios of Key West and Kone Foundation's Saari Residency in Finland. She is a graduate of the Boston University Creative Writing Program. After seven transatlantic moves between Finland and the U.S., she lives in Brooklyn and writes mainly in English.